Long Books, LLC presents:

Dragon Fang and Tiger Claw

Volume II

Tiger Claw

By E.Z. Drell

This is a work of fiction. All characters, organizations, and events portrayed in this novel are either products of the author's imagination or are used fictitiously. Any resemblance to actual events, locales, or persons, living or dead, are coincidental.

TIGER CLAW: DRAGON FANG AND TIGER CLAW VOLUME II
Mundelein, IL 60060
www.longbooksLLC.com
Released in the United States of America
ISBN: 979-8-9923419-1-1

"Tiger Claw" is the second entry in the "Dragon Fang and Tiger Claw" series. The first entry is called "Dragon Fang." Stay tuned for further entries!

Dedicated to those who keep fighting, even though no one else believes them or believes in them.

Contents

Chapter 1

Onigawa

Zeshiro and Aurabos traveled for days. The dry wastelands of *Onigawa* stretched for miles in every direction. The miasmic magenta clouds brushed this way and that by the wind like a purplish fog. It obscured their vision. The only hint at a trail they had was the rotten smell of the thousands of moths they hoped would lead them to the demon lord.

Follow the insects Master Tei had murmured before he died at the battle of Koga Temple one month ago. If this mass of moths were any indication, Zeshiro reasoned they were on the trail. "The foul smell of the moths reminds me why I left Onigawa in the first place," he coughed. "Ash and Kazi had to have left for similar reasons. There's so much misery in this wretched place. Even the air here is nigh unbreathable." The pair of demons, Ashnardzendegoff and Kaziastrazoff had been killed before the Battle of Koga Temple, but not before they had laid waste to the home of the Iga ninjas at the Battle for Iga Temple. Riku of the Koga and his team of Iga ninjas were able to destroy them with the very same legendary sword Zeshiro now held, Dragon Fang.

In the weeks they had traveled, they stopped only to catch their bearings. Being demons, they required no sleep and no food. Zeshiro wore loose white and gray robes around his muscular stature and a golden mask that hid his mouth and nose. The rest of his face was obscured in shadow other than the red glow of his eyes.

"My duty to protect the swords placed me in the human realm," the stone demon responded. Aurabos was large in stature. His body consisted of sections of sandstone wrapped in scaled samurai armor of white with black and red accents.

"You were guarding them in that underground cavern for *how long?*"

"Mm. Centuries. But I was awakened only when intruders entered. Now it is my duty to protect the bearers of the swords. That is why I follow you and for no other reason."

"So, if I lose Dragon Fang, you'll leave me alone? Seems like a fair offer if I didn't need it to kill the demon lord." The legendary blade, hilt woven in violet and black, hung in its sheath from his belt and had not left his reach since they entered the demon realm. They trudged further and further. Zeshiro had lost his bearings and constantly had to remind himself that the laws of nature were different here. He occasionally looked up at the silhouettes of the rocky landmasses that floated high above. Sometimes they were so vast that they obscured the sky. They made sure to be wary of floating islands directly above as rocks could split off, fall to the ground, and crash like meteorites.

"I'm glad we haven't run into any demons while we've followed the trail. Who knows what lies ahead?" Zeshiro said.

"Many of them have terrible temperaments and dangerous, unpredictable qualities. Best we avoid them if possible."

"Can you clear a path again with the wind sword? The fog irritates me."

"Yes," said Aura. He drew his samurai sword, a curved *katana* blade of considerable length with its white woven hilt. He gave a heavy downward slash with such force that its gust split apart the magenta fog ahead of them. It revealed a small stretch of wasteland. The visibility of some more space provided a small dose of relief.

"Stop," Zeshiro paused and held his palm in front of Aura. "I think I hear something."

"Is it the moths?"

"I don't know but...it's headed this way! Run!" They ran to the far end of the clearing until they reached the fog and then kept running. Ahead of them, a mass of moths swirled. They stopped. Zeshiro cringed at the terrible stench of mold they encountered. He covered Dragon Fang's handle with his hand.

"Ahh Zeshiro. My esteemed pupil," a voice spoke. The moths swirled until they coalesced into the shape of a bent old man. He carried a polished wooden walking stick with a score around the top third. His skin was tanned from too much sun. His eyebrows and the patch of facial hair below his lip were silvery white like the moon. "I see you recovered Dragon Fang. Well done, well done."

"Yes," Zeshiro said. He took a step closer to the old man while his hand still covered the curse-breaking sword's handle.

"And you killed the man guarding it?"

9

"Yes," Zeshiro lied. Riku had freely handed the sword over to him. He took another step closer. Only a few more steps and he'd be within striking distance of the old man.

"That sword is too dangerous to exist. It must be destroyed."

"Yes." Another step closer. Just a bit further.

"Soon my reach will extend beyond Onigawa. The human realm shall succumb to chaos and then I will make my move."

"No." Zeshiro pulled out Dragon Fang and swung it clean through the old man from hip to opposite shoulder. But it felt as if he had swung through nothingness.

"Fool," the old man said, smiling. "I knew of your betrayal the moment you set foot into Onigawa. You will die just like the humans you've sided with. Now, let's see you escape from here alive." The old man snapped his fingers and he dissipated into a cloud of thousands of moths that fluttered wildly in all directions.

"An illusion," Zeshiro said. "He's lured us into a trap." The ground shook as they heard the thuds of giant footsteps approach. Aura whirled the wind sword toward the sound. It revealed a bipedal golem four stories tall made of sandstone. With each of its steps, the ground quaked. It reeled back and slammed the ground with its rocky fist that sent a shockwave of earth in all directions.

They narrowly avoided the crash of the stone fist, though the shockwave tossed them back. They struggled to find their feet. "Let's get out of here!" Zeshiro called. Aurabos did not need to be told twice. He lifted himself up and with heavy steps started to run away with Zeshiro alongside him. The lumbering stone monster, though it took slow crashing steps, was right behind him. They stumbled with each footfall. "We're not gonna get away! We must fight!" They slid to a stop and about-faced. The massive stone figure came to a stop before them. It reached behind itself and brought its mighty fist down with a hard slam.

Without thinking, Zeshiro leapt onto the massive arm. As the monster straightened again, he hopped up onto its shoulders which lifted him four stories above the ground. He struggled to hang on as the monster tried to shake him off. The shaking took the monster off balance and it loaded all its weight onto one stoney leg. Aura took this opportunity to slash at the monster's ankle. The force of the air was so strong that the stone monster toppled face down to the ground. It gave out a deafening roar all the way down. Zeshiro barely hung on as he braced for impact. He climbed onto the shoulder blade as the monster crashed down. It struggled, flabbergasted because it had never been felled before.

"Finish it with Dragon Fang!" Aura called.

"Right!" The monster tried to push itself up off the ground. Zeshiro made his way to the neck and plunged the sword deep into the sandstone. In an instant, sand exploded in all directions. When the dust settled, Zeshiro stood and breathed heavily. His white and gray robes were covered in sandy dust. Aura stomped toward him.

"Now he knows we're after him," Zeshiro said. He watched as a stream of moths fluttered away into the eerie magenta fog.

Chapter 2

The Spot

In the human realm, Kwan sat alone at the spot where her lover died. It had already been a month since the destruction of Iga Temple, though to her, it might as well have been yesterday. Unomichi's death was all she thought about every minute of every day. From sunrise to sunset, she sat at the place he died. The flames of the spirit dragon *Noroi no Owari*, Curse's End, are what killed him. Unomichi had been cursed by a demon from the portal atop Mount Kyokushin and was unkillable, or so they thought. Whenever his limb was cut off, a new one grew back. Whenever he was stabbed, the wound closed on its own. Whenever his bones broke, they healed themselves. But the cleansing fire burned him to ashes just the same. And now, Kwan was left heartbroken.

Never before have I opened my heart to a man like I did with Unomichi. And I never will again. This grief...it is unbearable. He was so kind, so thoughtful, so brave. And now he's gone. How could the Spirits be so cruel as to take my love away from me?

Kwan was a thin, fit *kunoichi*. Her black hair, narrow eyes, and soft jaw made her appear quite beautiful by most men's standards. In days past, she would often wear colorful robes with beautiful flowery prints. But now she wore only the black robes of a widow with her white slip underneath. She used to keep her black hair in a tasteful ponytail or done up with pins and hair ties. Now, she just let it hang messily down to her shoulders without so much as a brushing.

Every day since Unomichi's death was the same. She woke up, threw her robes on, and resisted the protests of Takashi and Nobu. Then, she walked to her spot, knelt, and remained there until the sun went down. Takashi was Iga Temple's spiritual guide, and Nobu was her squad's captain. They would both approach and attempt to convince her to let his death go, but she couldn't. Flashbacks of the ephemeral dragon haunted her dreams every night. Each time it was the same vision. Unomichi laid down on the ground next to her. The dragon soared towards them ever closer until it opened its mouth wide and blasted them with holy fire. Then, she would wake up in shock and gasped for breath.

At first, Takashi said the memory would fade after a few days. Then, he said it would fade after a fortnight. But a month had passed and still she suffered the same vision night after night. She clutched the legendary sword Tiger Claw in its sheath closer to her chest whenever the pain was too great. It was the only comfort she had left. Her servant Gung Lao learned not to disturb her while she meditated at her spot in the stone courtyard. She had instructed him to wait at the spot for her and hand her the legendary sword. He was to bring her a plate from the dining hall at mealtimes and show himself away.

Gung Lao was a muscular retainer. He was a former slave from a distant land. As a child, he had been stolen from the home he didn't know the name of. Years ago, the Iga had rescued him and several other slave children during one of their missions and he had chosen to join them. He had naturally tan skin. When he was not attending Kwan, he spent his time exercising. He was so muscular that he had to cut the sleeves off all his robes so he could move his arms. Servants were treated well at Iga Temple and without disdain. It was not a bad life for them. Kwan found him handsome. She even considered offering him a place in the ninja-corps but that would mean he would leave her side. She wouldn't have that. He was the only one she could confide in. Gung Lao told her that, underneath, he was delicate. The thought of taking a life mortified him, the sight of blood froze him. He could think of countless things he would rather do than fight. Kwan and Gung Lao regularly exchanged their secrets. Years ago, when Kwan asked him if he was interested in her romantically, he replied that it would ruin their friendship, so the matter was forever off the table.

The people of Iga Temple were busy at work rebuilding their castle. Grandmaster Jin had ordered a large portion of the treasury to be spent on rebuilding fortifications and a new bell tower to replace the one the Corrupted had burned down. He sent messengers to collect stonemasons, woodworkers, and other builders to reconstruct the temple's castle walls. Iga Temple was built into a mountainside. The north side of the temple was the steep side of the mountain and the south side consisted of constructed gray stone walls built along a sheer drop. At the western entrance was a stone archway built into the castle walls. Zigzagging ramps led down to the forest below. It was easily defendable and deadly to assault. The main entrance stood on the eastern end. Armed guards were posted day and night atop the barricades. At least two men watched the comings and goings from there while two more stood just outside the painted red steel gate. All day, the gate remained open and it closed after sundown. Merchants and townsfolk were allowed to pass through during the day to conduct business with the temple denizens. Lately, many noticed Kwan as she meditated at her spot. She faced the entrance but did not pay heed to any one of them.

"There's that kunoichi again. She hasn't moved from that spot," travelers said as they pointed her out to their children. "One day she'll turn to stone."

"What's wrong with her?" the little ones would ask.

"I don't know. Must be heartbroken. Or it's a punishment. Or maybe she's an invalid. Who's to say?"

Kwan paid no attention to the townsfolk. *They wouldn't understand anyway* she thought to herself. So, she continued to wait at her spot. *Oh, Unomichi. Please return to me. I need you. I need you. Please come back.* Tears came and went from her weary eyes.

Her quarters were in disarray. Clothes lay all over her furniture. Bugs and rats took up residence in corners where trays were left half eaten. A musty smell filled the air. Kwan did not pay it any heed. After Gung Lao brought her back to her room, she would drift back into bed, pull the covers over her head, and try to fall asleep. She tried to forget the stench, and the sight of the rats just made her feel worse. Many times, Gung Lao offered

15

to clean the room for her, but she felt she did not deserve a clean room and waved him off, so it remained filthy.

After he recovered following the Battle for Iga Temple, Grandmaster Jin assumed leadership of the Iga ninja clan. Grandmaster Rohan before him had named him successor many years ago in case something happened to him. As it turned out, something *did* happen to him during the battle. The late Grandmaster Rohan was well past prime fighting condition. He was a man in his late seventies and he stood against the formidable and monstrous demon Kaziastrazoff. The large demon, with his purple skin and sluggish, brutish strength was bigger than any being any human had seen. Grandmaster Rohan fought as hard as he could. He even struck many blows against him, though his efforts were to no avail as the demon could not be harmed by mortal weapons. With his mighty axe, Kaziastrazoff knocked him off his feet and finished him with a mighty blow.

Thanks to the efforts of Riku and his legendary sword Dragon Fang, Jin and all the Corrupted combatants that did not escape recovered from the curse of the Lesser Toxic Mark. Jin had the respect of everyone in the temple, especially his son Hiriko. Young Hiriko followed Riku into battle to retake Iga Temple along with his best friend Kasume and several others, Unomichi and Kwan among them. The fighting spirit of the people of Iga Temple was reborn under the leadership of their new Grandmaster.

/ / /

Riku sat before Grandmaster Minato in the office of Koga Temple's dojo. The people chose Minato to be the new Grandmaster of Koga Temple. He had been betrayed by their former grandmaster, Master Tei, or rather, he had been betrayed by the demonic curse that was placed on Master Tei. The terrible curse nearly wiped out the humans of the mortal realm. But through the hard work, blood, and a little luck of a team of Koga and Iga ninjas, they managed to triumph, though they sustained heavy losses.

Riku wore his day-to-day attire which consisted of black robes and comfortable shoes. The ninjas of Koga Temple kept their swords at hand, always ready to defend the temple.

Grandmaster Minato wore the traditional clothing of the head of the Koga ninjas: pearl-white ceremonial robes, although he had the tailor add his own flair with brown and orange zig-zagging patterns along the hem. It is said that Minato can transform into a man-sized hawk upon the full moon's light. But, *officially* no one had seen it in person. They sat across from one another with a knee-high dark oak table between them. As they sipped their chamomile tea they smiled at one another as old friends do.

"I can't believe you're finally the Grandmaster of Koga Temple, Minato-sama," Riku said.

"I can't believe it either. Are you sure I deserve this honor and not yourself? I'm not even sure I want it! On second thought, you can have it!" The two men chuckled.

"No, no, no, no, no, Master! It belongs to *you* now, not me!" More chuckles. The painted *fusuma* door slid open and a smiling

17

servant stepped in. She wore a traditional white servant *kimono* and a bright smile. She carried a wooden tray with a silver teapot and two porcelain teacups. She made her way around Riku, whose back was to the door, and placed the tray on the oak table between the two men. Minato stared at her the entire time with an equally bright smile on his face. He could not take his eyes off her.

"Thank you, Mikoto-san," Minato said. She bowed to them. When she turned to shut the fusuma door as she left the room, she locked eyes with Minato and poorly fought off giving a giggle and a smile before she slid the fusuma door closed.

"You're still a scoundrel and a dirty old man, Minato-sama," Riku jibed. The old friends chuckled.

"No thanks to you, you ruffian. You've only been married to Sakura for how long now? And you beat out every other suitor while you were at it. The savagery."

Riku thought for a moment. Talking about Sakura was bittersweet. His previous wife Yuuki had long since disappeared deep into the forest. After investigation, Riku's guilt had been ruled out, but the result of her disappearance, whether she was alive or dead, remained a mystery. There were still those in the temple that remained suspicious of him, though Minato was not one of them.

"It's been less than a month, Grandmaster." He looked down at the cup of tea in his hand and felt a complex mix of happiness, sadness, and regret. He didn't know whether to smile or to cry.

Perhaps misreading his friend's countenance, Grandmaster Minato took a big slurp of hot tea and said, "Cheer up Riku-san! You're a newlywed! You need to provide that woman with a beautiful life now! And of course, many strong sons."

"Yes, many strong sons indeed. Sakura and I have thought about making our first new addition to our family."

"There is always time. Your marriage is still fresh." Minato took another sip of tea. "There will be plenty of time to leave…these unfortunate thoughts of Yuuki-san behind and move on. It is difficult to hear, but perhaps this sequence of events was for the best. Remember, in training we've learned to ease our attachments to things outside of ourselves. The things we gather, the people we meet, they are impermanent, ever-changing."

Riku closed his eyes and took a long breath through his nose and out again as if to feel his thoughts of her dematerialize in his mind. He thought of a drop of water dripping into a still pool. Upon touching the water, it caused a ripple that drifted out in all directions. As he delved inside the swirling clouds of his mind, time stood still, if only for a moment. He slowly opened his eyes and reached with a shaky hand for another sip of tea.

Minato interrupted his moment of quietude. "A part of her will always be with you, but it is best to try to leave the past behind."

Riku looked away and shut his eyes as his chin began to tremble. He thought she'd be with him until they grew old together or *she'd* become widowed; he never expected to become a widower himself. He began to snivel. "Okay."

19

They each took a long sip of tea, then sat inside a dense silence. Minato could sense Riku's inner turmoil and could tell the younger man was on the verge of tears. Minato spoke, "It is vastly unfair, when we are young, to have the whole of our life's journey before us. We are shoved onto this path whether we'd like to be or not. It is a long, uphill road. It is rocky, weathered, and winding. We have no guide and no map with little sense of direction. Yet at every moment, we have ourselves and we must keep going. Because sometimes, *sometimes*, we get a little enjoyment out of all the walking along the way. We can never know where this path will lead, but at the end of it, we can look back and see how far we've come.

"The going is getting tough, Riku-san; so, we must keep going. We'll have another talk soon. There is something more we'll need to discuss."

Riku pondered for a moment. "Alright, Grandmaster. And…thank you for your counsel. We are fortunate to have someone so wise leading us."

"Well, it's true that I *was* Tei-sama's second-in-command for a reason, Riku-san," Minato said. "I did not *stumble* into wisdom. I had an excellent mentor. Tei-sama…*knew* things." The ninjas of Koga Temple knew that Grandmaster Tei, who became old and wise, discovered some terrible secrets…secrets they were better off not knowing. Tei was the one that discovered the portal at Mount Kyokushin's peak, the same portal that terrorized the ancient forests of Japan and the villages therein.

20

The gentlemen finished their tea. Sharing a cup during meetings was a tradition Minato decided to continue. It was a delicacy Master Tei would partake in regularly during his long tenure as head of Koga Temple.

Riku performed a bow from his knees before the new Grandmaster, then stood and left the chamber.

/ / /

"You need to eat something, Kwan-san," Nobu nudged the kneeling *kunoichi's* shoulder. "And it's time for bed." As Kwan knelt at her spot near the middle of the courtyard like she did every day since the battle of Iga Temple, she looked up over her shoulder at Captain Nobu and stood while she grasped Tiger Claw in its sheath with her left hand. The sheath bore a beautiful design. Vermillion flowers flowed along the black background with tasteful subtlety. Its color palette matched the legendary sword's tight vermillion and black handle weave.

"And so it is," she replied soullessly as she gazed through Nobu's face as if she talked to a ghost. Nobu took her by the hand and guided her toward her quarters on the left side of the courtyard.

"Rebuilding Iga Temple has been a challenge, but we've made a lot of progress since the attack," Nobu said to her.

"Mhm," she responded, mind still lost in thought. Nobu was used to her half-responses. He was finished encouraging her to talk more. Children played in the verdant gardens on either side of their granite stone path. It brought a smile to his face. To his surprise, Kwan smiled at them too.

"I know his passing has caused you to feel...upset...Kwan-san. But Unomichi-san wouldn't want you to suffer like this. He would want you to move on with your life."

Kwan stopped and looked deep into Nobu's dark eyes. "I failed him," she insisted. To Nobu, the surrounding noise of the wind and the children that laughed and played died away. "He ordered me to protect him...and I failed him."

Her response unsettled him. The coldness of how she said it froze his skin. She said next to nothing to anyone since the Corrupted army's attack which was led by two terribly powerful demons. They nearly destroyed the temple.

"All I have left," she continued, "is to wait until I die so I can be with him once more and apologize for my failure."

"Kwan...I..."

She came alive, "There's *nothing* you can say to make this better, Captain. Nothing." The sounds of the wind picked up again. "Now leave me alone! I don't want to hear your poisonous words any longer today. Good night."

Nobu's jaw tightened. A fierce wave of anger boiled his blood. It was all he could do to not slap her over the head for her insolence. "Enough, Kwan-san!" he fumed. "I order you to stand down and...and get yourself together! And stop acting like a blasted child. Now go!"

She scowled at him and stole towards her quarters. She only paused to pull open the heavy metal door. She jerked it open and slammed it closed behind her. She left Nobu with the door's sound of a thunderous *clang!*

Indignant, Captain Nobu stormed off. He was unprepared to deal with deeply depressed female ninjas grieving over the death of a loved one.

Chapter 3

Best Friends Forever

"Akari-chan, finish up with those dishes! Now!" the innkeeper's obese head mistress, Onoka, screamed at the young girl. "The customers are waiting! You don't want to keep them waiting, do you?! They pay for your clothes and the food we feed you. You don't want to go hungry, do you?" The little girl frowned and returned to the dishes. She scrubbed them as furiously as she could manage.

"No, Mistress," Akari said though she did not look up.

"That's a *good* Iga mouse," the mistress said with a grimace as she struck the little worker over the head with a collapsed *ogi* hand fan. Akari rubbed the spot on her head but got soap and water all over herself. She began to sob silently as the mistress walked away. Mizu, a little girl slightly older than Akari looked over her shoulder at her. She folded towels that were "clean" and moved them from one mountainous pile to another then back again.

"It's gonna be okay, Akari-chan," Mizu said.

"No. It's not, Mizu-chan," Akari said as she fought to speak through her sobbing. "It's gonna be forever."

"It's not gonna be forever, Akari."

"Yes it is."

"No it's not," Mizu said.

"Yes it is."

"No it's *not!*"

"I double-dog *dare* you it is," Akari said. She began to smile.

"Well, I triple-*cat* dare you it's not!" Mizu replied.

"Well, I triple-double-*tanuki* dare you it is!" The two giggled between themselves.

"Well, I triple-double-quadruple *pinky swear* that it's—" Another mistress barged into the kitchen.

"What are you two giggling about?" This one was thinner and wore a tight-fitting jade dress with clashing crimson embroidery sewn on and usually had a less severe temperament toward the pair of them. Akari liked her better than Onoka, although she despised all the adults she came across at the inn. Akari didn't even know what the inn was called since she was left there by Riku, Kwan, and the others over a month ago.

"Nothing, Lee-san," Mizu said as she turned back toward her towel project.

"After you're done with your cleaning, I'll let you two go up to the roof tonight and look at the stars..." Mistress Lee said sweetly. Their faces brightened as they paused and looked at one another. "I'll even let you have some snacks."

"You're just the best Lee-san!" Akari yelled. This made Mistress Lee smile.

"Okay then hurry up and finish those dishes Akari-kun. It's getting dark out." She backed out of the room still in a smiling daze.

"Did you hear, Mizu?! Did you hear?! We're gonna see the stars! Isn't that great?!"

"What did I just tell you, Akari? It's not gonna last forever!"

"I can't wait for the stars! Oh, and the snacks! What kind of snacks do you think we'll get?"

"I want cookies," Mizu said.

"I want chocolate," Akari said. "Mmm. Chocolate."

The two girls went back to their chores, Akari scrubbed more vigorously and Mizu folded more intently than ever before with the image of going up on the roof to see the stars stuck in the forefront of their minds. Soon it would be Akari's ninth birthday. She hoped Mizu remembered.

Mizu was already on the roof outside their bedroom window when Akari met her there. The slanted emerald roof shingles were flat enough to sit comfortably on. Akari found Mizu nibbling on chocolate chip cookies as she gazed up at the sea of stars above. Mizu heard Akari climb through the window and onto the roof. She didn't look up.

"Akari, come look! The stars!"

"Oooooooh. They're so pretty," Akari said to her friend.

"What's that big white splotch up there? It takes up almost the whole sky!"

"Hmm, I don't know! Maybe the spirits spilled the stars and left them there?" Akari guessed.

"Or maybe there's so many that they make one *big* splotch!"

"That's stupid Mizu-chan! It's just a splotch!"

Mizu looked at Akari.

"You're stupid! Akari-chan."

"No you're stupid, Mizu-chan."

"You're stupid."

"No, you're stupid." They giggled. In between giggles they picked on each other and ate more cookies under the stars.

"Are we gonna be friends forever, Mizu-chan?"

"No, we're gonna be *best* friends forever, Akari-chan. Deal?"

Without a thought, Akari said, "Deal." She bit another cookie as she smiled at her friend and looked back up at the splotches of stars.

"I just...My mother used to let me stay up and watch the stars with her. I can't stop thinking about her," Akari said. "I don't know where she is or what happened to her. I miss her." Silent tears welled up in the corners of her eyes. Mizu looked at her and noticed Akari's tears. She put her arm around her.

"It'll be okay, Akari-chan. I promise. She's probably just looking up at the stars too and wondering where you are. You've been gone a long time."

Akari sniveled and wiped away the tears. "Yeah it's been a while now. I just hope I'm not in trouble. She gets mad when I misbehave."

"This is different though," Mizu said. "You were running for your life. She'll understand. The big monster scared you away from home."

"You're right. It was a big scary monster. He was purple with black horns and dark smoke all around him. I ran for my life...I should've brought my mother with me. What was I thinking?"

"Oh, Akari-chan," Mizu said. "It'll be okay." They looked back up at the stars and sat silently for a moment.

"I hate it here Mizu. We need to run away. You can come with me. Back to Iga Temple."

"Maybe one day, Akari-chan. Maybe one day."

/ / /

In her room, she sat upright in the fetal position. Kwan rocked anxiously back and forth. She couldn't sleep. The nightmares of Unomichi's death painted images across her eyelids whenever she so much as dozed off. Late into the night, she finally drifted into sleep. She whispered aloud *Michi…Unomichi… Uno…michi…no…no…Unomichi-san no…no don't…*

She gasped and sat up, wide awake. Disoriented, she looked around her room. It was dark, but her eyes—adjusted as they were to the darkness—could see the vague shadows of her bedroom. She heard what she thought was a vague echo.

Your fault Kwan. Startled, she looked around to try to find where the voice came from.

"Who…who's there? *Who's there?"*

It's all your fault Kwan. He died. Because of you.

"No! No it was not because of me! It was not!"

Yes it was, my dear. It was you. It was your fault. It was all your fault. Say it.

"No…it was…not my…It was all my fault. It was my fault. It was me. It was my fault."

It was all your fault Kwan. He died because of you. It was your fault.

28

Tears rolled down her cheeks as she muttered to herself. She sobbed as she laid back down and rocked until the darkness lulled her to sleep. "My fault," she said. "My fault."

She awoke late into the morning. She propped herself up with one arm and looked at her pillow. It was soaking wet. The hem of her white shirt was rough to the touch from the moisture. It bothered her neck. *I must've cried myself to sleep again,* she thought sullenly. *I'm just not getting out of bed today.* She plopped her torso back onto the bed and closed her eyes.

A chubby man opened the heavy steel door that guarded the entrance. He swung it silently until it was fully opened and gave a few brusque knocks that rang through the room. He wore a white shirt covered with a black overcoat and matching long black pants. He wore spectacles and the hat of a medical ninja.

"Kwan, it is time for a late breakfast. Actually, it's time for lunch. You missed breakfast again."

"Not now, Takashi-sensei. I'm busy." She rolled over facing the stone wall, her back turned.

"Come now, Kwan, you know how Grandmaster Jin feels when we sleep all day. Up during the day, down during the night. Up with the sun, down with the moon. It's only natural for us to ”

"Give it a rest, Takashi-sensei. I don't feel well." She adjusted her blankets and shut her eyes harder as if it would encourage him to go away. She thought to herself that she wished he'd drag her out of bed. She was enveloped by her melancholy a little too much to get up by herself.

As if he read her mind, Takashi walked to her bedside, grabbed her by the arm, and yanked her out of bed. "You're not wallowing in darkness today miss. Not on my watch." She protested a bit but stood up straight and looked at Takashi's feet. She meekly kept her arms close. He handed her some fresh clothing provided by the servants.

"Now put these on, Kwan. You are an Iga ninja! Not a cowardly mouse. Am I right or am I wrong?"

"You're right, Takashi-sensei…" she said. "But I feel so—"

"Don't say it. You'll render it real. Now get dressed and let's get the day started, soldier."

"I don't want to Takashi-sensei. I don't want to! I want to stay in bed and sleep. It hurts so mu—"

"What did I just say, Kwan?" Takashi asked, knowing the answer full well.

"That if I say it—"

"You'll render it real. Right. So, don't. Am I clear?" he asked. She nodded. "Okay then put your clothes on and let's go."

With that she vigorously put on the white shirt he handed her and went to her closet. She brushed the colorful oranges, crimsons, azures, and jades out of the way and pulled one of her black tunics out. She wrapped it around herself and walked out of the room as Takashi led the way.

As they walked past the gardens on either side of the granite path, Takashi said, "Now are you going to join us for drill practice today or are you going to mope in that same spot?"

"I'm going to do whatever I want, *Takashi-sensei*."

He said to her, "Know your place, Kwan. I'm here to help you. If you bite the hand that feeds you, you will starve to death. Now go mope in your spot. Turn to stone."

She ran away from him towards her spot. *Right where I left you* she thought as she approached it. Gung Lao waited there and held Tiger Claw. He always did whatever she said. He only answered to her, for better or worse.

"I kept it safe for you, Mistress. I've waited for you here all morning. Did you sleep well? Or was it the voices again?"

"I… I slept okay, Gung Lao. Thank you." Gung Lao bowed low and presented the legendary sword to her. She took it and knelt.

"Did you ever meet Unomichi-san, Gung Lao? I can't quite remember."

"Mistress I have not had the pleasure. During the attack when he was briefly here, I hid in the back with the families. I'm just glad the Corrupted never found us. You know how much I hate to fight. The sight of blood…I hate it."

"You best get over that fear soon, Gung Lao. When push comes to shove and your life is in danger, it is you or them. Remember that."

He gave a long sigh. "I will, Mistress. I will." He bowed and showed himself away from her spot near the center of the main courtyard where the incident happened.

Captain Nobu looked across the courtyard with a worried gaze as he saw Gung Lao bow to Kwan and jog away. "I don't know, Takashi-sensei. I don't know if she'll ever get better."

31

"She'll get better, Captain. She will snap out of it. One day, once her *yin* balances with her *yang*, like a coin toss landing on the opposite side, it will appear as if she was never melancholic at all. That is the way of things. It just takes time," Takashi said as he gave the same worried gaze.

"Okay. If you say she'll get better, then I'll believe you," Nobu said, trying to convince himself.

"Exactly. Now, just support her as best you can. Keep checking in with her daily."

"It's so frustr—"

"I *know* it's frustrating Captain!" Takashi interrupted. "But melancholy of the mind and the breaking of the heart take time to heal. Her balance will one day be restored once again. Just wait." The captain gave a sigh.

Chapter 4

Ninjutsu

The Koga ninjas that returned from Mount Kyokushin reported no issues with the demons of the portal. Going to the portal on top of the mountain was always a deadly venture. To make the journey, they would climb the weather-torn stairs and uphill pathways that led through the red *tori* gates until they reached the top. The tori gates had words painted on them in *kanji*: *Warning, danger ahead.* The ninjas had to ignore all thirteen gates climbing to the top. Once they reached the peak by dusk, the two ninjas would take their stances and wait for the full silver moon to sit on the horizon. Then, a rupture in space would open and two demons would emerge and the ninjas had to dispatch them. Riku had done it several times by this point in his thirty-two years, fifteen instances of which he'd been an official ninja of Koga Temple. The troubling part was that the demons *could* carry a curse, and in that case, whoever killed the demon with the curse had to be killed themselves. It was such a rare occurrence that the ninjas hardly worried about it, though it did take up space in the back of their minds. Regardless, to go to the portal was more of a chore than anything.

Riku awoke in his bed at Koga Temple and rolled to his right. He bumped into Sakura's body as she slept. He still wasn't used to sharing a bed with a wife. She wore her pink silk robe as she slept that went down to her thighs. She was blessed with the ability to sleep like a stone. Riku had a lingering sense of paranoia that caused him to be a light sleeper. It came with being a ninja. Usually, he awoke with the sunrise.

He gave Sakura a nudge. "Sakura. Sakura-chan, time to wake up."

"What is it, dear?" she said with her eyes closed.

"It's time to get up," he whispered. "The sun is rising. I must train."

"Oh, okay dear. Let me make us some breakfast." She stretched her arms past her head and gave a long yawn. Then, she turned around, leaned over, and planted a sweet kiss on her husband's lips. She looked into his eyes with a smile then got out of bed.

Yatta! I'm glad I married her, Riku thought to himself after he kissed her and smiled back. *I didn't even have to ask.*

Riku remembered how Yuuki used to bicker and moan whenever he asked her to do regular wifely chores. She much preferred to chat with the temple servants. She always wanted to argue about petty things like dishes and who would make breakfast. It always gave him a headache.

While his bride prepared breakfast, he did some light stretching and hopped into the ice bath. The chilling cold shocked his body, but if that was the worst thing that happened to him all day, then it was a good day. He scrubbed the sleep away.

"Riku-san, breakfast is ready!" Sakura called.

"I'll be right there!" Riku called back. He got out of the tub, water tumbling off him, and dried off. He put on his robes and shared breakfast with a smiling Sakura.

"Sakura, how are you always so happy?" Riku asked while they sat across the little breakfast table they had.

"I'm so happy all the time because I married you, dear husband. You make me so happy just by being you!"

Whenever she said things like that, it melted his heart. Riku had seen some terrible things happen around him in his past: ninja brothers killed, temples destroyed, long and dangerous journeys, and life-or-death situations. The worst was when Riku had to kill someone. Those were the ones that really bothered him.

"You're something else, Sakura. You really are not like other kunoichi in Koga Temple."

"No, I'm just like them," she smiled coyly. "I'm just the one that caught your attention."

"Well, you are the prettiest girl at the kunoichi corps." This made her smile and giggle. Sakura had a soft temperament. But if she was threatened she was as fierce as a tiger defending her cubs.

The lovebird newlywed ninjas finished their breakfast as they chatted and laughed with a little kissing mixed in.

"Come now," Riku said. "It's time for our training. You can't get by on *just* your good looks, my dear." She giggled and gave him a playful hit on his arm.

As they left their apartment, which was built into the rectangular temple structured around a vast courtyard, they held hands and gazed into each other's eyes. He kissed her and said, "Be safe, my lady Sakura. I'll see you again tonight."

"Okay. I'll see you then, my love," she said softly in return. Riku ran off between the gardens of Koga Temple toward the training ground.

I can't wait to get back to her, he thought as he ran. When he reached the training square, he saw Hiriko and the others gather for the first of two daily practices.

"Right on time as usual, Riku-sensei," Hiriko said. "How do you do that?"

"Raw talent, young Hiriko-kun. Raw talent." The two of them laughed. Hiriko was a tall ninja known for his extreme dedication to whatever he put his mind to. He was from Iga Temple, but he had become a valued member of the Koga.

"Kasume is late again. He's always eating too much and sleeping too much and making a fool of himself. I think you or Grandmaster Minato should straighten him out before it's too late." Hiriko always thought his best friend did not take life seriously enough, though Kasume would always say Hiriko took life too seriously.

"Sure, I can talk to him, Hiriko-kun." The other ninjas stretched and prepared for training to start. "Listen Hiriko-kun…"

"Yes Sensei?"

"This is part of your training: you need to relax a little. You need to take a deep breath and appreciate the joys of life sometimes. Too much intense exercise will ruin your body and mind. Remember this."

"So…my training…is to…not train? I do not understand sensei."

"When Kasume-kun arrives, go with him to the market and buy some snacks. What's your favorite snack Hiriko-kun?"

Hiriko raised an eyebrow. "So…I can't do physical training today?"

"Answer my question. What's your favorite snack?"

"Umm…well I guess I like mochi…what does this have to do with training?"

"Just listen! Take Kasume-kun and go to the market. Get mochi. Enjoy the day. That's an order, soldier. Now hold out your hands." Hiriko did it. Riku reached into his pocket and pulled out 5 silver pieces, way more than enough. "Spend all this money on whatever you want at the market."

Kasume came strolling to practice at that moment. "Sorry I'm late Riku-sensei. I—"

"I don't want to hear it right now Kasume-kun. Now, go with Hiriko-kun to the market. He will brief you on your mission."

Kasume assumed attention stance with his legs together and stood up straight, chin high. "Yes sir! Let's go Hiriko." Hiriko looked at Kasume and back at Riku, then back at Kasume.

"This is the weirdest mission I have ever—"

"Now *go* Hiriko-kun. One more complaint about your mission and I'll tell Minato-sama you've disobeyed a direct order."

"Sorry sensei, sorry. I'll go with Kasume. Sorry sir…" Hiriko went to Kasume and the two of them ran off.

The rest of the Koga ninjas assembled. They each wore a white *gi* and their respective belts of various colors. The eight black belts took up the front row followed by each rank further down in the preceding rows. The black belts trained in front so the colored belts could use them as role models for how ninjas should behave.

"Stand at attention!" Riku ordered. At once the ninjas obeyed. Each carried their wooden *ninjato* training swords and held it vertically against their body with the tip pointing downwards and both hands on the grip. Riku was appointed by Minato to be the instructor. He nicknamed the troupe "Team Riku" after the team that defeated the Corrupted army a month and a day ago. Some of the Corrupted Koga were still in the infirmary. When the Lesser Toxic Mark curse was broken, after Master Tei was slain by Dragon Fang, their corruption faded rapidly.

"Today we will perform the traditional *ninjutsu kata* forms from beginning to end, all twelve of them in succession without stopping. Go up to the highest *kata* you know, colored belts. Do them until you've used all your energy, then do your highest kata once more." Riku heard a few sighs. This only made Riku smile to himself.

"Kata now, sigh later. Now—*begin!*" The ninjas sprang into action. The black belts began immediately and the colored belts, especially the young white belts looked to each other for what to do.

"Um…excuse me sir…Riku-sensei…" a young white belt said. He was no more than six years old.

"Yes Ren-kun?"

"Um, well I don't know what to do…" Riku chuckled a little.

"Yellow belts!" Riku called for the yellow belt sisters who were six and seven years old respectively.

"Yes sir?!" They paused what they were doing and stood at attention.

"Show little Ren-kun here one of the white belt kata. *Ka No Kata*, if you please."

Without hesitation they responded curtly, "Yes Riku-sensei!" The younger sister Sana motioned for little Ren to join them. The older of the yellow belts, Yoko, took her place in front of the other two and led them through the kata motions.

After watching the trio go over their white belt kata for a minute, Riku joined the black belts. Each black belt was allowed to practice whatever they felt they needed to practice.

Iito, Master Tei's former right hand was nowhere to be found ever since a few weeks before the Corrupted attacked. He was disciplined, deadly, and would be classified as a murderer had Master Tei not backed him. Being in his presence gave Riku the chills. Iito would be useful to have on one's side since he was so powerful a killer, but he could not be trusted. His absence was appreciated.

"I've been training my jump, Riku-sensei," said Daisuke, one of the black belts. Riku felt Daisuke was a great leader. He had a pleasant temperament but was also very lean and strong.

"Make sure you pull your knee up high. Your body goes as high as your knee. Remember that Daisuke-san."

39

"Yessir, thank you sir." He proceeded to jump as high as he could. He drove up his knee like Riku said.

Another black belt named Goro motioned for Riku's instruction. He was the heaviest out of all the ninjas but he also had the strongest strikes and was more able than any of them to focus his *chi*. Riku came over to him. "Sensei, I need to do lots of exercise today. I want to do some running, but it's so tiresome."

"I'll run with you, Goro-san. Come now. We'll do a lap around the courtyard." Goro sighed and the two of them began running along the perimeter. Goro took slow, heavy steps but he ran as best as he could.

As they began to run around the vast rectangular courtyard surrounded by the likewise rectangular temple building, Riku noticed Minato emerge from his quarters at the northern end.

Panting, Riku said, "Goro-san, you go on ahead. I'll catch up." Goro groaned but kept running and dragged his feet as he went. Riku came to a halt before Minato. He approached and said, "Is something on your mind, Grandmaster?"

"Riku-san. It is time we spoke once more."

"Very well, sir." He caught up with him and followed close behind. As they made their way to his office, the Grandmaster said, "I have a mission that is sure to interest you deeply."

"Oh? And what is this mission?"

"Not here. We'll discuss it once we reach my office."

He followed Minato warily through the dojo. It had pale-green *tatami* matted flooring over the square area used for ceremonial purposes. It was also where the black belts were allowed to train with Grandmaster Minato during rainy days.

They reached the office. Minato usually enjoyed his tea in this smaller room while visitors came and went, asking for advice or permission. Sometimes he would spend time with company there. This was not one of those times.

The two men sat down on the *zabuton* cushions, resting on their heels. "Riku-san, Tei-sama gave us a cryptic message just before he died. Do you remember?" Minato asked.

"Of course, Grandmaster." Riku replied. "He mentioned there is a demon lord threatening the forest."

"Yes. And we have seen no other sign of this demon lord. This troubles me. It is as if this wretched being is biding his time, waiting for the perfect moment to strike."

"Hm," Riku contemplated. "That is troubling."

"Yes. Rather than simply remaining vigilant, I have decided we do something about it."

"...Go on."

"Legends tell of a hidden scroll residing far away that could give us an advantage against such a foe."

"And where is this hidden scroll?" Riku asked.

Minato's female servant Mikoto entered the room dressed all in white with a wooden tray with two teacups and a teapot.

Minato waved her off, "Not now Mikoto. Not now. Thank you, dear." The woman looked stunned since the Grandmaster had never refused tea before. She gracefully bowed, still holding the tray.

"Yes Master. Do you want the tea later?" she asked meekly.

"But of course, Mikoto! I adore your tea," Minato said. "But not now, thank you." Riku looked up over his shoulder at her as

41

she backed out of the room. Another servant that waited outside the room closed the fusuma door behind her.

"Riku-san. Our scouts reported the hidden scroll I mentioned resides in the shrine atop the frozen Hokkenzen Mountain. It is a very dangerous task to reach it."

"And I'm to retrieve this scroll?"

"Yes. You are to retrieve it. Then, you are to use it at the shrine to bring Unomichi-san back to life."

"Oh? Unomichi-san?" Riku said. He would have choked on his tea if he had any in his mouth. *Now there is a name I'd rather have remained buried in the past.* "How would I go about doing that, Grandmaster?"

"The scroll contains a secret technique that only a wielder of a legendary weapon can understand. I do not know how it works. That is why I need you to reach the shrine and discover the secret technique. You are to use it as soon as possible. That is your mission. I expect one of you to leave, and two of you to return."

Riku mulled over the order for a minute. "Traveling to Hokkenzen Mountain would be quite an ordeal. Do you mean I will be traveling all that way alone?"

"Well, I suppose that would make it a little too challenging," Minato began. He paused, then said, "You may select a few others whom you trust to accompany you. As usual, the nature of your mission must be restricted to only those who must know. If this lurking enemy discovers your mission, he could take measures to disrupt it."

"Yes Grandmaster. Understood."

"Now, who will you select to bring with you?"

"Hmm…I'll need a day to think about it, Grandmaster. If this mission is as dangerous as you're making it out to be, it is imperative I choose someone I trust. Also, I need to consult my wife. Is it okay that I tell her?"

"Can she keep it secret?"

"I'd trust Sakura with my life."

Minato looked to the side at the Midas sword resting horizontally on its stand and mulled over the request for a moment. "Then I'll trust your judgement. Yes. You can tell her."

Riku smiled and took another bow as he said, "Thank you, Grandmaster. She is one person I cannot lie to."

"Yes, thus is the hardship of being a man. We can keep little secrets and it is written all over our faces, but women can keep *big* secrets without even a hint of deception. That is the nature of things."

"You're wise, Grandmaster. And I pray you soon meet a woman that will keep big secrets from you. You've been without a woman for too long."

Minato sniffed. "Well, being frozen in gold precluded me from experiencing any romance, my friend." They chuckled.

"What of Mikoto? I see the way you look at each other."

"Well, Mikoto is my servant. She is very beautiful, and I may very well be in love with her, but would it not make things…strange between us if I were to fumble with my words in front of her?"

"You're the *Grandmaster of Koga Temple* sir! I'm sure she'd understand if you fumble your words a bit."

Minato smiled. "Riku-san I don't know how you do it, but you have the charm that can make an old witch turn friendly."

"You flatter me."

"Now, come back at daybreak tomorrow morning and let me know whom you've selected to go on this journey. I'll brief you with more details then."

"Yes Grandmaster," Riku said as he bowed low again. He stood up and exited the office quarters.

He thought to himself as he slid open the fusuma: *Spirits, a frozen mountain? This should prove to be a difficult mission. And all to bring back Unomichi, huh? I know someone who'd be thrilled about that if she could ever look me in the face again without scowling. I've heard Kwan has never been the same since the night of the attack. And who could blame her? She thought she finally found the love of her life. It's a shame it had to end how it did. Knowing Unomichi, he would gladly give up his life a second time if it meant saving the ones he loved. And I feel the same. Sakura-chan will no doubt be angry with me for taking on such a precarious mission.*

Chapter 5

The Laughter of Children

Midday saw the sun high in the sky up ahead. Dead leaves brushed across the ground and made a satisfying crinkling sound, but Kwan hardly noticed. She waited for something to happen as she knelt at her spot. She clung to Tiger Claw and kept it close to her chest.

Unomichi-san. My Unomichi-san. My one love. Come back to me. Unomichi-san...

She sat on her knees as she rested on her heels in her black ceremonial tunic. She had long since lost the feeling in her calves. She had specifically requested this funeral tunic to be made for her against many angry words of protest from Captain Nobu. She did not know why she did not just kill herself to be with her dead love, Unomichi. Her stubborn heart was too weak to join him in death. As she was lost in thought, a little girl no older than seven years old ran around her and stood on the spot of his death, looking lady Kwan in the face.

The little girl twisted back and forth in playful nervousness. Feeling perturbed, Kwan looked at the girl. "Um... err... what is your name little one?" Kwan faked a smile for her. *It turns out I'm not completely heartless.*

"Jyuni, Mistress Kwan," the little girl responded. She kept twisting back and forth. "Captain sent me."

"And…what does the captain want? Speak." The little girl frowned at what she thought was a mean response. "Err…sorry Jyuni-chan. Why did Captain Nobu send for me?"

Jyuni shrugged. "He said you're too sad. Why are you sad? It's nice out today. Be happy. Why can't you be happy?"

Shocked at the child's bluntness, she fumbled to respond. "Well, Jyuni-chan…when a man loves a woman. I mean when a woman loves a…when two people love each other and one of them…er…goes away forever…the other one is left sad… and…"

Without hesitation, Jyuni said, "Well where did your lover-man go? Why did he go away forever?"

"Well, he didn't go away forever… he kind of… well you see… Jyuni-chan how old are you?"

"I'm six-and-a-half. Well, six-and-three quar-ers. My mommy said I'm six but really I'm six and almost seven. So that's why I say I'm six and a half I mean six-and-three quar-ers. How old are you Mistress Kwan?"

The naivety of the little girl put a real smile on Kwan's face. "I'm twenty-seven and three-quarters, Jyuni-kun," she said with a giggle.

"Wow you're really old!" Jyuni said incredulously.

At this Kwan laughed out loud. She laughed and laughed. She was beside herself with laughter.

"What's so funny Mistress? Why are you laughing?"

Kwan couldn't stop laughing. She hadn't laughed this hard in a month and three days. "It's…It's nothing…It's nothing Jyuni-chan. You remind me of myself when I was your age." Her giggling calmed down and she had completely forgotten her melancholy. She looked around to see if anyone noticed. Gung Lao approached. "Mistress what's wrong? Why are you smiling so fervently? Captain Nobu has been looking for you."

"Gung Lao this little girl put a smile on my face just now," she said joyfully. She turned back to the little girl. "What's your name again little girl?"

"My name's Jyuni, Mistress Kwan. I'm six and three quarters and I like to hop, skip and um… I like to dance too."

"Isn't she funny, Gung Lao?"

"She is very funny. Whatever you say Mistress. She's just a child," Gung Lao said as he misread the situation. "Now, Mistress, will you come see the captain?"

She stood and turned. In her left hand she held Tiger Claw still in its sheath. Jyuni's eyes lit up as she noticed it. "Ooh! That's a pretty sword! Can I see it? Can I? Can I see it?" She held her hands to her chest with hope.

Kwan could not let this girl down. She turned to her and said, "Of course little swan." Kwan held Tiger Claw horizontally and grasped the handle with her right hand. She pulled it out. She revealed the ninjato sword, triple claw marks on the blade and all.

"*Ooh!* It's so pretty, Mistress! Can I swing it? Can I? Can I swing it *please?*"

"You can swing it when you're old enough, Jyuni-chan."

"*Aw,*" she said disappointedly. Kwan saw her frown and swung Tiger Claw toward the air at their side. A puff of fire emitted from the slash.

"*Yay! Again! Again! Again Mistress! Again!*"

Kwan put Tiger Claw back in its sheath. "I'll show you again tomorrow, Jyuni."

"Mistress, the captain is waiting," Gung Lao interrupted. A group of little boys and girls ran by. Jyuni took one more look at Kwan and she ran to catch up with the group of children.

The tracts of grassy gardens in Iga Temple's grounds were perfect for children to run around in. Some of the girls brought dolls and toys. The boys liked to imagine they were ninjas, just like their fathers. They would take sticks and try to beat each other with them while the girls sat, played with their dolls, and talked. Sometimes the boys would drag the little girls into playing with them, to much protest, though they did it anyway. Whenever it was boys versus girls, the girls always ended up screaming playfully as they ran away.

As the children played, a man dressed all in black walked onto the green. The kunoichi watching over the children turned and wondered who it was. He did not look like a ninja of Iga Temple.

Sensing danger, she gathered the children and herded them away back to their individual families' quarters.

"Where is he?" the man in black demanded.

"Where is who, sir? And who are you?" the kunoichi said.

"Where is the one they call Riku?" his calm voice grew angry. "*WHERE IS HE?*"

"I don't know who you're talking about, sir," she said calmly. "There's no one here by that name. You should leave the temple immediately if you're going to cause a stir. You'll scare the children."

"I have no time for this..." he said. He rushed the kunoichi. She pulled out the knife she carried with her and tried to stab him in the abdomen as he approached. He caught her arm and tackled her to the ground. He held her wrist as she tried to struggle away. He bashed her head again and again. "You should've told me where he is." He revealed his own dagger and plunged it into her heart. With a scream and a gasp, the kunoichi was dead.

Captain Nobu heard the scream and ran with his ninja students toward the danger. They were on the far side of the courtyard. *IT'S IITO! MEN! SOUND THE ALARM! WE'RE UNDER ATTACK!*"

Iito stood up off his victim and bolted toward the temple gate. Twelve guards gathered between the charging perpetrator and the gate entrance. They brandished their steel short swords.

When Iito approached them, he launched two hidden *kunai* at them. Two guards were struck in the neck and died as they hit the ground. The rest of the guards surrounded him. He ducked under a guard's horizontal slash and retaliated with a fierce axe-kick, knocking the man out. Then he drew two swords from the sheaths on his back. Nine more to go. The new temple bell roused the temple for the first time. Time was running out for Iito.

He threw one of his swords and sent it spinning like a sideways pinwheel. It chopped the fourth guard's head off before he could react. Two guards attacked him from behind. He deflected both strikes and landed a hard side-kick into the chest of one of them. He knife-hand struck the other in the neck before he stabbed him through his light leather armor. He couldn't dislodge his own sword out of the fallen guard so he wrestled free the dying man's sword. Then he leapt and stabbed another guard's back as he came down. Six down, six to go.

Iito pulled his bloodied sword out of the man's back. A wave of something hot hit him from behind. *Fire?!* he thought as he danced in alarm.

Kwan stood nearby with Tiger Claw and a fierce disposition on her face. "*Enough, Iito!*" she shouted. She stood in a deep defensive stance and gripped Tiger Claw's hilt with both hands.

Iito rolled around on the ground where there was enough dirt to douse the flames. He stood up, his burned clothes in tatters. The other guards backed up as the two ninjas faced each other. Iito's skin was singed but he was more than alive.

"Where is he, rat?" he yelled in a fierce fashion. "Where is Riku? Or do I have to kill you too?"

Kwan slashed Tiger Claw to the side that burned a fiery path to her flank. It was a warning slash. "He's not here, you monster. Now go. Run. Leave Iga Temple now."

"I won't run. My master is a demon lord. He wants Riku's head."

"Well, you're not gonna find him here. Riku is dead. He died at the attack on Koga Temple a month ago."

50

"Don't lie to me, you pitiful vermin. I know very well Riku is alive." The burned ninja spat to the side. "Now tell me where he is before I destroy you."

"I'm not telling you anything, demon-man."

"Why do you protect him, young lady? Do you not know that he's a murderer? He even killed his closest friend, Unomichi. You know him, do you not?"

Kwan gasped. "You know of this? *How do you know this?*"

Sensing he struck a nerve, Iito continued, "Yes, yes, Unomichi-san. Riku killed him—his best, life-long friend—he killed him mercilessly and with pleasure. I was there. He had a smile on his face as he killed him."

"You're a filthy *liar*, Iito. You're a man of no honor at all. Demon."

"No, I am not. You witnessed it yourself. Yes, now I remember you. What is your name again, miss?"

Nobu and the rest of the ninjas he was training across the courtyard approached with their wooden practice swords in hand. "Kwan what is going on here?"

"Don't say anything to him, Captain! He's a demon-man!"

"Ahh Kwan is your name. Thank you, Captain," Iito said deviously. "Kwan, come find me if you want to know more about why Riku killed Unomichi like he did. But first I must take my leave. Hopefully you understand."

The guards that surrounded him braced for impact. Before anyone could react, Iito took a pellet out of his pocket and slammed it on the ground at his feet. With a deafening *bang*, black smoke burst from the compact explosion. The ninjas and guards of Iga coughed and covered their faces. When the smoke cleared, Iito was gone.

"Damn it all!" Nobu cursed. "He got away."

"Who was that, Captain?" one of the ninjas asked.

Nobu sighed and said, "That was a rogue ninja named Iito." A shudder blew through the guards and ninjas present like a stiff breeze. "He is one of the descendants of Shō Temple. No one knows what happened to the survivors after their temple was destroyed almost a century ago. It appears someone has been training the survivors in forbidden arts."

"Forbidden arts, Captain?" Kwan inquired. "What kind of forbidden arts?"

"I can't tell you. That's why they're forbidden!" he scolded. "Now quick; get the medical corps here," Nobu ordered. Two ninjas in training ran off to get the medical experts.

Nobu shook his head. *So…Iito has returned. I hope the stories about him are not true. One can only hope…*

"Captain," Kwan asked, disheveled. "Why did he say Riku *enjoyed* killing Unomichi?"

"Iito is a snake. He'll say anything to get to you."

"But Riku…how much do we really know about him? Maybe he *is* a sadistic murderer like Iito said. What then?"

"He's not. It's a lie."

"But do we *know* this, Captain? Do we know this?"

The captain sighed, "Kwan, get some rest. We'll talk about this later."

Dissatisfied, Kwan thought, *I must know. Riku could have killed him intentionally. Or at least, didn't hesitate to sacrifice him. That mighty spirit dragon he summoned—Noroi no Owari. Surely it could've spared him! I must know.*

Kwan bowed to the captain and took her leave. Rain clouds gathered above and a vague rumble announced the storm to come.

Chapter 6

Selections

"Gung Lao," Kwan addressed her servant. "Prepare my things. We're going on a journey." She and her servant were in her quarters the day after Iito's attack. It was early afternoon and they had just returned from the dining hall after they had some beef and vegetable stew.

"Mistress, you're not thinking straight. You are under Takashi's supervision. If he—"

"I don't care if he finds out!" Kwan snapped. "If you're not going to gather my things, I'll do it myself!" She grabbed an armful of clothes and stuffed them into her travel bag along with small water jugs and some *kunai* throwing knives.

"Mistress I am sworn to protect you and go with you wherever you sojourn. But we don't even know where Iito disappeared to." He crossed his arms. "I advise against this."

"Fine. Stay here Gung Lao. But me? I need answers." She grabbed Tiger Claw off the rack where it rested horizontally and strapped it to her hip.

"Mistress…" Gung Lao wanted to object even further but knew it was futile. Once Kwan made up her mind about something, there was no stopping her. The best he could do was go with her. "Where will you go? We don't have any clue where Iito went."

Kwan thought for a moment. "We should first check Prima Village at the base of the mountain path. He had to have gone through there. If he's not there, we can try somewhere else. Perhaps we can check Koga Temple. Riku will be there. I'll face him myself." She glanced at Tiger Claw at her hip and massaged the vermillion and black woven handle. It vibrated just enough for Kwan to notice. *What's wrong, Tiger Claw?* she thought. She could swear the sword could read her thoughts. It was a legendary weapon whose purpose, she learned from Aurabos, was to defend its twin Dragon Fang. The two swords being separated for this long caused Tiger Claw to seem restless, at least, that is what she felt the sword communicated to her.

Do you long to be with your brother? she asked in her head. Tiger Claw rumbled a little. *Dragon Fang was entrusted to the demon Zeshiro, though. It's impossible, Tiger Claw.* It shook some more. She remembered what a rigorous challenge it was to procure this sword and its twin. The deep darkness of the cave, the giant bat monster, the thorn pond, and not to mention the formidable stone demon guarding the chamber of the swords. If not for Unomichi and Tiger Claw, they would've been killed in that sword chamber by the relentless dead.

"Are you okay, Mistress?" Gung Lao asked. "You've been staring at your sword for a little too long now." Kwan snapped out of it.

"Of course, Gung Lao. Now, tell Takashi-sensei we'll be leaving immediately."

"Right away, Mistress," he replied reluctantly as he bowed, fist over his heart. He left her quarters.

55

We'll find out soon, Tiger Claw. We'll know for sure if Riku intended to kill our love. The sword calmed.

/ / /

Riku strolled around his ninjutsu students as he inspected them. It was a warm day and they had practiced their techniques for two hours in the training grounds in the courtyards of Koga Temple. The black belts worked on silent running while the colored belts worked on their *kata* forms. Over and over, they'd perform the same precise movements. The colored belts prepared for their promotion tests which were coming up in two weeks. Hiriko and Kasume were slated to test for their black belts. Kasume was worried he would not succeed, despite Hiriko's reassurance that he would be fine. Hiriko was confident that he himself would make the full rank. The training at Koga Temple was similar to the training of the Iga, though his father Grandmaster Jin urged him and Kasume to train under Riku-sensei.

"Riku-sensei is the best ninja warrior I have ever met," his father had said to him. *"It would be wise to train under him to further hone your skills. Also, it will temper you to be away from home. I know Kasume would feel right at home with the Koga as well."*

"Focus, Hiriko," Riku called to him. "And Kasume, remember to tighten your abdomen as you strike during your *kata.* Imagine you're fighting someone as you strike. Don't discount the power of your mind."

The pair of them refocused and continued their training. Riku gazed at the pair of them, then looked over at Daisuke and Goro. As they silently ran around the training gounds, Riku thought, *I need Daisuke and Goro to lead the instructions in my absence, so they're out. Hmm who then shall I bring?* He paced around the practice square arms crossed. There were of course the other master ninjas of the temple, but his mind drifted toward Kasume and Hiriko. They had proven themselves during the battles at the temples and perhaps they would prove useful again.

"Kasume-kun. Hiriko-kun. Come here," Riku motioned. The friends paused and looked at each other before they ran toward their sensei. "You two are coming with me on a mission."

Kasume's face lit up. "Oh, a mission! I love missions!"

Hiriko gave Kasume a smack on the shoulder. "No you don't Kasume. You never fail to start complaining halfway through."

"Shut up, Hiriko. No I don't," Kasume said as he glanced over at his friend, then back to his teacher. "What's the mission, sensei?"

"You're not gonna like it, Kasume. Our mission is on Hokkaido."

Hiriko crossed his arms. "You mean the snowy island to the north? What could we be doing there?"

"I need you to accompany me on a retrieval mission. There is something I need to collect. It rests in Hokkenzen Shrine."

"Hokkenzen Shrine?" Kasume asked.

"That's known as the most difficult shrine to get to," Hiriko said. "People have died trying to get to it. It's on top of a frozen mountain."

"Indeed. If you accept the mission to come with me, I'll award you with your black belts." Their faces lit up. "There will be many tests along the way."

"I'm in!" Kasume said.

"Kasume, you can't just jump in like that! You must think about it first," Hiriko jibed.

"I *did* think about it! I'm in!"

Hiriko gave an audible sigh. "If he's in then I'm in too. How soon before we depart?"

Riku said, "We leave at daybreak in two days. We need to make some preparations. However, it's a secret mission. That means you can't tell anyone where we're going. Understood, Kasume?"

"Aww," Kasume replied disappointedly. He liked to brag about his adventures to the Koga ninjas he barely knew.

"I won't tell anyone," Hiriko promised.

/ / /

Kwan and Gung Lao departed from Iga Temple at sunrise. Gung Lao carried their light bags over his broad shoulders. He wore a dark sage shirt that could barely contain his strong physique along with khaki shorts that came down to his knees. He liked to wear clothes that would help him blend into the surroundings just in case he needed to hide.

Kwan walked delicately in her black robes with vermillion flower print and Tiger Claw strapped to her left hip. She meant to find Iito and learn more about Riku. He must have gone through Prima Village. The little town was nestled near the base of the mountain trail that led to Iga Temple. During the attack a month ago, Team Riku was in such a dire rush to save Iga Temple that they didn't even stop in the village for supplies. Although Riku was a Koga ninja, he and his fellow Koga brother-in-arms Unomichi joined with a squad of Iga ninjas. Kwan and Captain Nobu were among them. Dragon Fang and Tiger Claw in hand, they were initially headed to Koga Temple to vanquish the curse of the toxic mark. After they found Iga Temple destroyed, Team Riku decided to confront the Corrupted invaders in the castle. It was a conflict which, although successful, came at the cost of Unomichi's life when he succumbed to holy fire breathed by the spirit dragon Noroi no Owari under Riku's control. That same fiery breath vanquished one of the demons that led the enemy invasion. After the battle, the team went on to Koga Temple and eradicated the curse when they defeated the corrupted Master Tei.

The mountain path curved along the side of the mountain. Gung Lao liked to look over to the south at the trees which stretched all the way to the horizon. He thought it was lovely how the morning sun over the mountainside that stood along their left gave a soft glow to the treetops. Kwan kept her eyes forward while she was lost in thought. Her mind often drifted somewhere else as it carried her between the sadness of her lost lover and her new motivation to find out about his killer.

"Iito must be in Prima Village," Kwan said. "I have a feeling." As late morning approached, they reached the small town. Prima Village was a group of cottages in concentric circles that surrounded the town square. The plaza was constructed of brick flooring with a central firepit. Vendors would come to the market in the square selling rice, spices, fruits, and vegetables from their wooden carts. Sometimes they would even have meat. Iga denizens would often come to the village for supplies. Usually there were a few guards from the temple assigned to patrol the village.

"Excuse me, Mistress," a little boy tugged on Kwan's robes. He could tell by her fancy attire, at least by the village's standards, that she was from the temple. The little boy was filthy and sickly looking, like he had been neglected. "Do you have some money so I can buy rice for my mama and papa?"

"Of course, child. Gung Lao, give the little boy a few bronze coins."

"Yes, Mistress," Gung Lao swung the bag from over his shoulder, rummaged a bit, and pulled out a handful of coins. He gave the little boy three bronze coins, enough to buy a big bag of rice. Before the little boy ran off, Kwan knelt and grasped the little boy's shoulder.

"What's your name little one?" she asked. The boy didn't respond, he just looked down and away, clearly wanting to leave. "Little boy, do you know where the elders of the village live? I must ask them something." The boy looked over his shoulder and pointed to a cottage across the town square. The cottage was larger than the ones next to it, though still a humble little home.

It had clay shingles the color of copper with white molding and a heavy metal door like at the temple.

The little boy ran to a group of men standing near a merchant's wooden cart. The men wore swords at their hips and wore ragged, filthy clothes. Kwan watched as the little boy held up the bronze coins and handed them to one of the five thugs. The man snatched the money out of the little boy's hand and struck him over the head, taking him off his feet. The little boy wallowed on the ground for a second before he wiped his tears and got up.

Gung Lao looked at Kwan. "Mistress, I think we've just been robbed."

"I don't care about that Gung Lao, what of that little boy? We need to help him."

"But what can we do, Mistress? Those thugs have weapons. There's five of them," Gung Lao said. He looked at her sideways. "Surely you don't mean to cause a scene…Mistress, we need to pick our battles. This has nothing to do with us."

"I'm picking this battle, Gung Lao. It's not about the money. It's about principle. Besides, these thugs will scatter like loose grass in the wind. Watch." She stomped toward the thugs. She looked back over her shoulder as Gung Lao looked at her incredulously. "I'm an Iga ninja, Gung Lao. I can't stand by and watch the weak get abused. Not on my watch."

"Just don't get hurt, Mistress."

Kwan marched over to the thugs while her left hand covered the handle of her prized sword. She stopped twenty feet before them as they laughed and bickered with each other and paid her no mind. On closer inspection, their weapons were not swords, but machetes instead. "Excuse me, that money belongs to me," Kwan called to them. She looked at the ground in between. Silence, if not for the breezy, warm early autumn wind that blew through the area. A swift gust of air rolled across the empty space. It blew dust and debris across the brick ground.

"Who are you, stranger?" one of them said.

"It's our money, get lost," said another.

Kwan responded, "The little boy: does he belong to any of you?"

The men chuckled, "He's part of our crew, lady. What did you say your name was?"

"I didn't," she said. Another warm breeze swept across the square. Onlookers watched in anxious anticipation. After a pause, Kwan said, "If you raise the boy to be a poor thief, then a poor thief he will be. If you raise the boy to be a good man, he'll make you rich beyond measure. The choice is yours."

"What're you talking about, lady? Do we have to rough you up?" The five thugs looked at each other and readied their machetes. The little boy ran across the square to Gung Lao and hid behind him. He peeked around his thigh. The large man couldn't watch. He shielded his own eyes with his hands.

"I do not wish to fight you, only to show you the error of your ways."

"*The error of our ways?* What, are you some sort of do-gooder? You speak like you're an Iga ninja."

"What if I were?" she said coldly. She cracked a grin and looked up at them. She narrowed her eyes.

"You're not though," one of them said. "And I'm going to show you what we do to troublemakers around here. Show him, Shizugi." The most unhinged of the bunch stepped forward, machete already drawn. He was scrawny and disheveled. He had a wild look in his eyes as he looked from side to side anxiously as he approached.

The leader of the troupe called from behind him, "Shizugi has killed many people, big and small. You'll be no different. Kill her, Shizugi."

Shizugi ran at her wildly and swung his machete in wide circles as he closed the distance. As he approached, Kwan watched him closely. When he got close enough, she dodged his predictably wild swing, stepped past his right side, and in one quick motion, pulled out Tiger Claw and cut the ruffian in half diagonally from hip to shoulder. The two halves of Shizugi fell to the ground. The ruffians and the crowds that watched the scene gasped.

Kwan flicked the blood off Tiger Claw and slid it back into its sheath. The ruffians took frightened looks at each other. "Well, don't just stand there, *attack!*" their leader said. The remaining ones charged in much the same way Shizugi did.

As they charged, Kwan said to herself *Hm, they chose to fight instead of flee. I must punish them.*

Gung Lao knelt and covered the little boy's eyes. The first ruffian ran full force into Tiger Claw. Kwan pulled it out, blocked a wild slash from the second, swung Tiger Claw and chopped his head off. The third threw his machete at Kwan from a short distance. She deflected it with a strong side swipe.

63

Amazed it didn't kill her, the wide-eyed ruffian began to run away. Kwan closed the short distance and stabbed him in the spine, then she ripped Tiger Claw out of his side. Gung Lao, many paces away, retched.

Again, she paused and flicked off the blood. The final ruffian threw his machete down. And knelt before her. "Please don't kill me lady. I beg of you, spare me."

"Where is the one called Iito?" she said as she approached him, Tiger Claw held out in front of her.

"Iito? Wha-wha-who's that? I don't know anybody by that name! Please, don't kill me." She took a step toward the pitiful man.

"*WHERE IS HE?*"

"I don't know! I don't know!" he cried. "Please! Don't kill me! Please."

"You fool. Look at your comrades. Do you see what happens when you live like a thief? You get killed. If you don't tell me where he is, I'll have to kill you," Kwan said coldly.

The man began to sob, "*Spare me! Spare me, Mistress.*" The man prostrated himself.

The crowd, who was silent, began to yell, "Kill him! Kill him! He's a thief! Kill him!"

"The people want me to kill you. Why should I not?" The man looked up, tears covered his face, trousers doused in urine.

"I, I…don't kill me, please. I'll do anything. *Anything,*" he pleaded.

Kwan stood above him and spat at him. She began to walk toward Gung Lao as she put Tiger Claw away. After five paces, she stopped. The crowd chanted, "Kill him! Kill him!"

Kwan turned around and in one quick motion, pulled out Tiger Claw and sent a stroke of fire that engulfed the man in flames. On his knees he cried as he burned before them. His corpse fell facedown. Kwan walked toward Gung Lao as if nothing happened. She nonchalantly returned Tiger Claw to its sheath.

"Ready to go?" Gung Lao asked, shaking.

"No, we need to find Iito," she said.

"Well, if he was here, you've scared him off by that scene you caused."

An elderly woman approached them. She wore black garments and an equally dark hood. A flowery colorful bandana covered her hair. "Excuse me young lady, hmm, young man," she bowed, "but you made quite a spectacle, hmm. Those men have been terrorizing Prima Village for quite some time, hmm, and no one had done anything about it. Thank you."

Kwan bowed with a smile. "My pleasure, ma'am." She looked over to Gung Lao with a quick glance, then back to the old woman. "Excuse me, do you know the whereabouts of a man named Iito? He wears all black like a ninja, but not like that of the temple. Partially burned. He has a dangerous demeanor. Do you know of him?"

"Hmm, I haven't heard of a man named Iito, no, hmm," the old lady said. Kwan and Gung Lao looked at each other disappointedly.

The little boy, still at Gung Lao's side spoke up. "Iito? I know Iito."

The two Igas looked at him. "You know Iito, little one?" Gung Lao said. The little boy nodded. "And where is he?" He pointed down the road outside the village.

"He came through the village, little one? Did he say where he was going?"

The old woman said, "Hmm, come to think of it, there was a stranger wandering the village, hmm. As I recall, he was asking around, hmm, about someone named 'Riku.' Wasn't Riku the one who killed the demons?"

"Yes ma'am. But he killed my husb—err," Kwan began.

"Hmm, your husband, Mistress?"

Kwan rubbed the back of her neck and instantly regretted her slip of the tongue. "Well, you see, we weren't *married*…exactly. More like *promised*; engaged if you will. It's complicated."

"Ahh I see. He killed your lover, hmm?" the old woman said coyly with a smile. "You must be out for revenge. Why then are you looking for Iito, hmm? Surely you should be looking for the killer. Riku is a man of Koga Temple, hmm, is he not?"

"Yes ma'am. But you see, Iito just attacked our temple and, well, he has answers about Riku-san. Answers Riku himself would not tell us."

The old woman thought for a moment. "Hmm, this seems like a trap to me. That man Iito was quite rude, hmm. He all but scolded me for not telling him what he wanted to hear! Ripped

66

the apple out of my hand, he did. Quite rude, he was. Hmm, quite rude."

"Did you tell him where Riku resides?"

"Hmm, well, I had no choice, I told him he lives at Koga Temple. But everyone knows that, they do. He's famous. What is an old woman to do against a fierce man like this Iito?"

The Igas looked at each other. "Thank you, kindly woman. Perhaps you can show the little boy some hospitality and look after him for a little while?"

"Oh, this little boy is a troublemaker, hmm, but I can have someone look after him. Don't you worry. Come, child." The little boy took the old woman's hand and kept his eyes on Kwan as they turned their backs and scurried away.

"Well, we know where we must go next. Koga Temple," Kwan said.

Gung Lao sighed, "Mistress it's three days walk from here. Can't we—"

"We're going," she said sternly through his protest.

"Yes, Mistress," he replied, defeated.

Chapter 7

Steady As She Goes

As Akari washed the dishes once again, she looked over her shoulder at Mizu who was lost in thought as she folded towels. The room they shared was cramped, humid, and warm. Akari regularly had to borrow towels from the stack to wipe moisture off her forehead. Mizu didn't mind. What was one more towel compared to the three mountains of them she had to get through, after all?

"Mizu, I hate this."

"Me too Akari. This stinks."

"How do we get out of here? Those adults left me here and all I've done is wash these stupid dishes. I hate washing dishes!"

"I hate washing dishes too, Akari," Mizu said. "I hate towels almost as much as I hate dishes."

Akari scrubbed her sponge against a dish. There was a green stain on this dish that was particularly stubborn. She scrubbed it harder and harder but it would not come off. "Let's think of a plan to escape."

"Shh, a mistress is coming." The young girls went back to their tasks. Akari scrubbed more vigorously than before.

The bigger one, Mistress Onoka, pushed through the double doors. "Stop bantering and focus on your tasks. Mizu-chan, finish that pile then you can go to your room. Akari, come here.

I need to talk to you." Akari quit scrubbing and gulped. Mistress Onoka never had anything supportive to say.

"Akari-kun, what is this?" She held up a dish from the rack with a slight water stain on the underside. "I told you to scrub these clean!" She slapped Akari over the head.

"I'm sorry Mistress, I..."

"You *what*, Akari-kun? I've told you time and time again to hand-dry the dishes before you put them on the rack. Did I not?"

"Yes you did Mistress..." Akari couldn't look the big woman in the eye. She was too scared. Hand drying them with towels just made more work for Mizu. Either Mizu was angry at her or Mistress Onoka was, and Akari preferred Mizu.

"So do it or I'm withholding your supper next time." The big woman turned around and pushed through the swinging doors to the inn proper.

Akari sighed and returned to her dishes. "We need to get out of here, Mizu."

"Yes we do, Akari."

"I'll think of something tonight," Akari said. She returned to her spot at the sink after she wiped the moisture off her forehead once again with her towel.

/ / /

Later that night, Akari laid in her bed roll next to Mizu's. The room in the attic of the inn had a large window that overlooked the jade-roofed town. It was a bigger town than Akari was used to.

69

"Mizu, how did you end up at the inn?" Akari asked. "You've never told me."

"You've never asked, Akari," Mizu replied.

"Well, how did you?"

Mizu began, "My parents died when I was very young. My father was a guard of the town here. Kyogama Town. Mistress Lee said my grandpa was a Shō ninja and he had much, much honor. Before he died he sent my father to live with my mother's family in the town here."

"Oh wow," Akari said. "You're a Shō descendant?"

"Uh, yeah I guess so. Doesn't help me much. I'm stuck here."

"Yeah," Akari said disappointedly.

"My mother was promised to my father when she was young and they were married as soon as my mother came of age. They had me soon after. And well…"

"You still didn't tell me how you ended up here, Mizu."

"Well, I don't like talking about it," Mizu rolled away from Akari and began to shed tears softly to herself, but she could not help but let out a whimper.

"What's wrong, Mizu? Are you okay?"

"Well…men came and…they…" Mizu said to the wall.

"They what?" Akari asked.

"They came and they killed my father in his sleep," Mizu said. "My mother she…well…I don't know what happened to her. Bad things. She died." Mizu fought back tears.

"Oh. I'm so sorry Mizu. I…I didn't know."

"Well now you do. I was on the streets as a three-year-old. Mistress Lee said servants found me crying in front of my house and took me in at the inn. I've been here ever since. Now, how did *you* end up here, Akari? You just showed up one day a month ago and you never left. What gives?"

Akari fell silent for a moment. She realized her friend had worked at the inn for her entire life. At first, she did not know how to respond. "Well, I lived with my parents at Iga Temple. I liked to arrange flowers from the gardens."

"Ooh you lived in Iga Temple? Why did you leave?"

"A big monster scared me away. I ran and ran and ran. I wanted to run forever. I tried to run to Koga Temple but I ran into a ninja troupe instead. They were Iga ninjas!"

"Ooh Iga ninjas?! I heard they're the strongest ninjas in the world! Did you meet Grandmaster Rohan? Or Master Jin?"

"No but I did meet Riku! And a nice kunoichi named Kwan. They were led by Captain Nobu."

"I've never heard of him."

"You've never heard of Captain Nobu?!" Akari said. "He's the leader of the best Iga ninja squad!" From downstairs they heard Mistress Onoka demand they keep quiet and go to sleep.

"Sorry Mistress Onoka," they called together. They brought their voices down to a whisper again.

"Anyway, they took me to the village and left me with Master Goshen and Lady Goshen who then plopped me at the inn after the pagoda burned down."

"I remember that! That was so scary!" Mizu raised her voice. "The giant tower burned down! I saw it from this window! There was that huge fight too!"

"Shh Mizu, Mistress Onoka will hear us."

71

Mizu lowered her voice, "Sorry. Okay so how do we get out of here? It's awful and I hate it. I've been stuck here my whole life and I wanna go."

"I've only been here for one month and I can't stand it anymore!" Akari exclaimed.

"Shh…Mistress Onoka," Mizu reminded.

"Oh, right. Sorry," Akari said as they giggled. "Now about our plan…"

"Well, we should go to a temple. Which way is Iga? Your mother must still be there, right?"

"Yeah she'd be there but I don't remember how to get there. I was so scared I just ran away without thinking."

Mizu gasped, "You don't remember? How do we find our way to Iga Temple then?" Akari fell silent for a moment. She rolled around before she uncovered her blanket. She stood up off her bed roll and looked out of the tall rectangular window that overlooked Kyogama Town.

"I don't know."

Chapter 8

Surprise

Riku, Kasume, and Hiriko gathered at the front entrance of Koga Temple. The main entrance held stations for ninja guards on the roof and on the ground floor. Unlike Iga Temple, which was akin to a castle built into the mountainside, Koga Temple was built on flat land amidst the Great Forest. Built within a grove, the wooden rectangular temple's corners fit nestled between the trees. The brown shingles that covered the roofs of the building sloped downward on either side which resulted in red trim all the way around. In the middle was a vast courtyard complete with dry and wet gardens and plenty of room for training. The Koga relied on the thick forest for protection rather than fortifications.

"Did you gather all your belongings yet, Kasume-kun?" Riku asked the young, short, stocky ninja.

"Yep," he replied. He felt around his person for his things. "I've gathered my ninjato sword, my kunai daggers, and I even brought some shuriken throwing stars. What about you, Hiriko-kun?"

"Well, I've secured my bow and a handful of arrows, plus my ninjato, of course."

"Very good, boys. Let's head out," Riku said.

"Riku-san! Oh Riku-san! Wait!" a woman's voice called to them. The three of them looked over and saw Riku's bride.

Sakura wore faded pink robes with flower print and a bandana with a pattern of many-colored flowers that covered her hair. She ran to them and carried a large woven basket. It threw her off balance and caused her to run awkwardly. "Riku-san! Oh, and Kasume-kun, Hiriko-kun, I brought you some rolls so you wouldn't go hungry. There's a surprise in the middle of them too," she said with a smile.

"Oh! Wow thank you so much, Sakura-san. They look tasty!" Kasume said.

"Thank you, Lady Sakura," Hiriko said with a bow.

"Give us a minute, you two," Riku said. He waved them away, which they obliged after smiling at each other. "Sakura-chan, these smell lovely." Sakura was trying hard to not break eye contact with her husband. Riku picked up on her nervousness. "Is there something bothering you, my dear?"

Sakura's chin trembled. "Husband, I have news. But I don't know if this is the right time."

"What is it, just tell me, Sakura." He came close and stared into her eyes. She struggled to look her husband in the eyes.

"Well, um, my stomach was hurting quite a lot. I had some terrible cramps yesterday morning. I asked Bokomi-sensei what it meant, and she said…well…"

"What did she say?" Bokomi, the head of the kunoichi ninja corps, was an expert healer. Sakura and the other kunoichi relied on her insight for their womanly needs as well as spiritual guidance.

Sakura took Riku's hand and placed his palm delicately on her belly. "She said I'm with child. I am pregnant, Riku. I'm a little scared." This time she looked in his face to see how he would react. Riku's face was blank other than his mouth hanging slack. A broad smile soon lit up his face.

"Don't be scared, Sakura-chan! I've wanted a child for so long. This is wonderful news!" Sakura's face lit up with joy. Riku held her even closer, closed his eyes, and kissed her deeply on the lips. A surge of positive emotions rushed over him. He separated from her by a step and cheered towards the heavens.

"*Yatta!* Oh, this is wonderful Sakura-chan! Wonderful!"

"I'm so happy you're happy, Riku! I have the best husband in the whole world!" she said with glee and the two of them hugged and laughed together.

"Hey, you lovebirds, what gives?" Kasume and Hiriko grew impatient near the gate.

"I'm going to be a father, Kasume-kun."

"Oh! Well, um...congratulations," he responded, not knowing what to say.

"Congratulations, Sensei. Many blessings upon your household," Hiriko said formally. "Congratulations, Sakura-san. May your child grow up big and strong, and with a full belly and a warm bed every night."

"Thank you Hiriko-kun. Kasume-kun." she replied with a bow. "Now, I have preparations to make for the pregnancy, and you three with your mission. You should all be going now. Be safe and make sure to mind your feet so they don't hurt so much on your journey. And be wary of strangers."

Riku looked at her and took her close. "I'll return to you, I promise."

"Okay," she said softly. "I want so badly to come with you."

"Out of the question. Even more so now that you're carrying our child. We can't risk it. And you can't tell anyone where we're going. Tell them we went for a routine patrol mission."

"Your secret is safe with me," Sakura said with a wink. He smiled back. "But husband, when will you return?"

"I don't know, Sakura-chan. It won't be too long." He turned to Kasume and Hiriko. "Let's go." The three of them adjusted their packs and turned to leave.

"Finally," Kasume said.

As they walked through the temple gate, Kasume looked back over his shoulder. Through the gate he could see the tended gardens of Koga Temple, maybe for the last time.

/ / /

Akari and Mizu had waited on their bed rolls for what seemed like forever. While they lay on their backs, the little girls looked out through the window at the night sky above. Akari saw hundreds and hundreds of stars. Some twinkled and some hung still. The night sky was so colorful with faint pinks, purples, and whites that streaked from one end of the sky to the other.

They waited an hour after they heard everyone go to sleep. "Mizu-chan, are you ready?" Akari whispered to her friend.

"Yeah I'm ready. Do you think we saved enough food?" Mizu asked.

"I hope so. I packed as many rolls and cakes as I could. I even filled some jars with water. We should be okay," Akari said. "You have the rope, right?"

"Yes I have the rope. This is going to be scary. We could get hurt."

"We'll be fine," Akari promised, mostly to convince herself. She had no idea how their escape would go, but she had to hope for the best.

They lifted their covers, stood up, and grabbed their packs. They climbed through the window out onto the roof. It was dark, but they knew the way. The jade roof shingles slanted downwards on either side. The apex that divided the roof was a solid platform about a foot wide, just wide enough for the girls to run along. The rest of Kyogama Town was quiet. The streets were empty. Lit torches from nearby buildings provided just enough light for them to keep their footing as they went along the roof. They struggled to keep their balance but finally reached the end. A statue of a knee-high chubby stone dragon capped the end of the long platform. Akari just hoped it was sturdy enough to hold their weight.

"Hand me the rope," Akari said to Mizu behind her. Mizu nervously handed it to her and continued to struggle to keep her balance. Akari tied it around the dragon statue and let the rest of it fall to the ground. Akari didn't hear it touch the bottom.

"I don't know if the rope is long enough," Akari said to Mizu.

"We must try anyway, Akari. I'm not going back to stacking towels." After a deep breath, Akari reached down and grabbed the rope. She swung around to the top of it and began to lower herself. She tried not to look down but could not help but sneak a peek. Her grip tightened and she gave a muted shriek. She was high up, but she had to keep going. There was no going back. She slowly lowered herself down. After she climbed down far enough, Mizu took her turn to swing onto the rope. Akari reached the bottom and dropped down. She came down with a crash and after she touched the ground, she fell to the side to take the pressure off her feet. It hurt, but she was alright. Mizu climbed down after and did the same. The two looked at each other and giggled for a moment. They got up and snuck around the back of the building. Akari felt her heart beat wildly in her chest. She finally felt free again. Silent tears of joy welled up in the corners of her eyes and she could not help but smile.

They snuck through the space between the inn and the protective stone walls of Kyogama Town. When they planned their escape, they thought about the gap between the inn's roof and the town walls, but there was no way. The distance between was too great, so they were forced to devise another plan.

They ran with all their strength through the alley between the buildings and the perimeter wall. There were tall, unmanicured patches of grass along the neglected dirt pathway. It wreaked of filth.

Finally, they reached the town gate. As they approached, Mizu whispered, "Akari-chan, how do we get past the guards?"

"I don't know! I didn't know there would be guards!"

"You didn't know there would be guards?!" in disbelief, Mizu exclaimed under her breath. Akari shrugged. They huddled against the last building.

"It looks like the guards are in the guard house," Akari said. "If we sneak past them, maybe we can escape."

They inched toward the gate. The three guards sat around a table and laughed. They were not paying attention to their duties. Akari thought she smelled alcohol. The two of them ran through the gate.

When they were safely on the outside of the gate, they made for the cover of the forest across the path. "I think they're more worried about people coming in rather than going out," Akari said with heavy breaths.

"Okay we've made it out of the gate," Mizu said, also breathing heavily. "Now, which way is Iga Temple?"

Akari looked both ways down the path. "It's one of the two ways. I think it's this way." She pointed down the northern way. "Hopefully we find the path to the temple along the way."

"Hopefully?!" Mizu exclaimed as she whispered. "This is life or death Akari-chan!" Akari swallowed.

"It's that way. I know it is." Again, Akari said it more to convince herself than her friend.

"It's spooky out here, we don't have anyone to protect us."

"We'll have to protect each other, Mizu-chan."

"Let's go. I want to get away from this place."

Chapter 9

The Jewel

Autumn was setting in and Akari felt a cool breeze when the sunrise finally peeked over the trees. The thick foliage of the forest made it impossible to travel on either side of the path. They had walked all night, still unsure if they were headed in the right direction. The stiff breeze blew dead leaves from one side of the path to the other. Every time the wind blew, Mizu gave a shudder. She was not used to being anywhere other than inside the walls of Kyogama Town. Akari, a little more well-travelled, hesitantly took the lead of the pair, even though she was the younger of the two. She still hoped that Mizu remembered that today was her birthday.

Once they saw the sun over the trees to their right, Mizu asked to take a break, to which Akari agreed. The girls found a small opening between the trees they could squeeze into with a little room for them to sit down comfortably. "Akari-chan, give me a second," Mizu said. She reached into her pack.

"What is it?" Akari asked. She felt her heart beat faster. Mizu dug around in her pack.

"I've been waiting to give this to you. I was thinking about it all morning." She grabbed something and closed her hand around it.

Akari's face lit up in anticipation. "What is it? What is it?"

Mizu opened her hand and in her palm was a thin black cord necklace hooked with a jade jewel. "I made this for you," Mizu said. "You're my best friend in the whole world. You're the only one that has ever cared about me. I want you to have this."

Tears began to well up in both of their eyes. Akari turned around so Mizu could tie it around her neck. Once it was secured Akari turned back around and squeezed Mizu. "I'll never forget you, Mizu-chan, as long as I live. You're my best friend in the whole world too." They hugged each other as hard as they could as they teared up with huge smiles on their faces.

"I'll always protect you if you'll always protect me, Mizu-chan. Do you promise?"

"I promise, Akari-chan. I promise. Happy birthday," Mizu said. From then on they knew they were in this together.

"Thank you, Mizu-Chan. Thank you," Akari sniffled. "Now let's have some cakes." They let go of each other and Akari pulled out the biggest cake roll. She broke it in half and the two giggled to each other and smiled as they ate. She pulled out one of the water jugs as well and took a swig before she passed it to Mizu, who took a big gulp. She sighed after she took a sip.

Mizu smiled and said, "I'm already much happier than when I was folding towels at the inn. It hasn't even been a full day of freedom yet."

"I know. Me too," Akari said. "I felt like a prisoner, and I didn't even do anything wrong!"

"Yeah! Mistress Onoka was always so cruel to me ever since I was put there when I was little."

"I know, she was awful. I don't know how you stood it for so long." Akari said. She took the bottle and drew another big gulp. "I might miss Mistress Lee though. She wasn't so bad."

"If you got on her bad side, she could be worse than Mistress Onoka, though. I say good riddance to all of them!" Mizu punched the grassy ground with her fist. "But they're gonna come searching for us when they realize we're missing."

"We'll be long gone by then," Akari said with conviction. It took very little to convince herself of that point. "We can rest for a little while but after that we must keep going. We don't want them to catch up with us."

"Right. That would be a nightmare," Mizu said. They rested for a little while. Akari fiddled with her new prized possession and smiled every time she felt the smooth gem. The jewel was the color of grass and was taller than it was wide.

"Where did you get this jewel? I've never seen it before."

"Mistress Lee said it belonged to my mother. Now I'm giving it to you, so take care of it!"

"I will," she replied with a smile. She shut her eyes and felt so relieved and secure with her best friend at her side. Tears welled up in her eyes that soon fell down her face.

/ / /

The waning crescent moon was low in the sky over Koga Temple. The day before, a messenger had come from Iga Temple that the murderer Iito was on the loose. The news troubled Grandmaster Minato whose first order upon hearing it was to double the guard day and night. Rumors of the news spread through the temple and caused unease that made it hard for many to sleep. The message included the information that Iito was searching for Riku, who had departed the temple the day before.

That night, Grandmaster Minato went to bed and clutched his *tanto* short sword to his chest. He found it difficult to relax but finally, he fell asleep.

As the silver crescent moon rested upon the tops of the trees, Minato awoke to the sound of his fusuma sliding open with a crack. "Grandmaster Minato! Wake up! Wake up!"

"What's happening?" Minato said groggily. He looked up at the Koga ninja from his bedding.

"We're under attack! Quickly! Get ready!" All feelings of grogginess were usurped by alarm as he threw his blankets off. Flustered, he jumped out of bed and did not let go of his tanto. They heard metallic twangs and yells of fighting in the hallways.

"Here he comes!" The ninja ran from the doors to the hallway. From his bed chamber, Minato saw a man in dark robes slaughter the ninja guard.

"Iito," Minato said to himself under his breath. "Iito!" he called to the murderous ninja. "Why have you come here? Why do you disturb the peace at my temple?"

Iito breathed hard and stomped toward the bed chamber. He never broke eye contact with Minato. "Tell me where he is," Iito said.

Minato knew who he meant. It could only be one man. He drew his tanto and held it underhanded between himself and Iito.

83

If he could stall for time, more guards would show up. But Iito was too fast. With a powerful, lightning-fast spinning straight-leg kick, he knocked the tanto out of Minato's hand. Without missing a beat, he turned and smashed Minato in the stomach with a sidekick. The kick pushed him back against his dresser and knocked things over.

Iito lost patience. He yelled with a rugged voice, "Tell me where Riku is or I'll kill you and everyone that comes in here!" Minato said nothing. It only made the rogue ninja angrier. Iito pulled out a dagger and held it with the point inches away from Minato's face.

"Okay! Okay. He isn't here. I sent him on a mission somewhere far away. He won't return for quite some time."

"Where did you send him. Speak!" Iito tightened his grasp on his dagger. His wrist pulsated from the exertion.

"I sent him to the northern island of Hokkaido."

"Where on Hokkaido?" Iito demanded. "Tell me! Or do I have to torture you?" He pressed the tip of his dagger against Minato's neck until a drop of blood escaped.

Minato saw no way out of this. It was either he told him, or he would die. "The frozen shrine of Hokkenzen. Now please, leave us in peace. If you leave now, I will call off the guards. There are dozens of them and you'll never fight them all off."

"Hokkenzen?" Iito said to himself. "But that would mean…fine. I accept your deal. Guide me out of here safely through the guards."

A ninja appeared at the door with his ninjato drawn and a scowl on his face.

"Peace, Daisuke-kun. We're escorting him out of here peacefully," Minato said.

"But…Grandmaster, he's badly injured many of us. You can't just let him leave…"

"I said let him go!" Minato barked. Daisuke stood frozen with a scowl painted across his face. He was conflicted whether to follow the order or attack the invader. After what felt like years, he begrudgingly sheathed his ninjato. He stepped aside as Grandmaster Minato, still in his night robes, led the dangerous man out through the hallway. Daisuke and Iito locked eyes as he passed while the former frowned indignantly. Servants tended the injured guards in the hallway. They looked up at their Grandmaster as he walked by with his chin held high. The perpetrator followed a step behind him. They walked through the gardens as onlookers watched them make their way to the entrance. When they crossed the outer threshold Minato stopped and Iito kept walking.

"What is your motive, Iito? Why are you looking for Riku-san?" Iito paused and looked back over his shoulder before turning to face him.

"My reasons belong to my master and I alone," he replied coldly. The word *master* did not sit right with Minato. He had heard of Iito and his history as a descendant of the Shō ninjas, but that clan had been destroyed long ago.

With a furled brow, Minato said, "Who is this *master* of yours? Your clan was destroyed a century ago."

He scowled, but did not respond. Then, he started northward along the path and left Minato behind.

"What is he planning?!" Minato called after him. Iito did not respond. The Grandmaster watched as the ghostly man disappeared around the bend. *Iito cut through our defenses like a talon through water. And his skin was disfigured. This cryptic master of his...it certainly warrants further investigation.* He shook his head and returned to the temple.

Chapter 10

Mist

When they were ready, Akari and Mizu packed their belongings and made their way back onto the path. They walked the entire rest of the day and bantered as they went. Mizu asked many questions about Iga Temple.

They came across several paths that led towards the mountains to the east or to the forest to the west. Akari wasn't sure which path led where, so they kept walking northeastward up the main path. Sometimes strangers dressed in robes passed them by with a lifted brow, but they quietly went on with their own business. They walked until the sun went down, still not satisfied they had found the path to Iga Temple. Akari had once run down this very path scared for her life while Iga Temple was under attack. She was too scared at the time to commit to memory anything of what she saw along the way. She just remembered running through the darkness, not knowing what became of her mother, or anyone else for that matter. "We should stop for the night," Akari said.

"Okay," Mizu said. It rapidly got darker and they could barely see. There was no easy opening in the foliage so they had to push their way through. Under the trees there was space for the two of them to rest. Mizu swung the pack off her back with a crash.

"Careful! We don't know how long we'll be out here!" Akari said. She slowly placed her pack on the ground.

"Akari-chan, where is Iga Temple? We've been traveling all night and all day. Where is it?"

"We'll find the path soon," Akari said, more to convince herself. She held back the tears. She knew the path had to be there somewhere. Maybe she'd remember the path when she saw it. "C'mon, let's eat something."

The darkness crept in and all the light they had was the starlight that filtered through the trees. Mizu took out four cakes and handed two of them to Akari who looked up at the stars. When Mizu nudged her with the cakes she looked down and took them. They took huge bites.

"I'm so hungry." Mizu complained.

"I'm cold. Do you know how to build a fire?"

"No, I've never even left Kyogama Town before."

"I don't know how either." Mizu came close to Akari and put her arm around her. Akari did the same. They laid down huddled together and tried to doze off to sleep. They were exhausted and frightened. Now and again, they heard the crunch of footsteps trudge along the path, and each time they looked up. Thankfully, the thick brush concealed them. The wind blew moist, chilly air through the brush. Mizu began to sob silently. Akari hugged her tighter and she too began to sob.

"Don't cry Mizu-chan, we'll be there soon," Akari said to her friend, trying to convince herself too. *I want my mother,* she thought to herself. Akari would not be able to sleep tonight.

It was breezy and chilly. Mist threatened to obscure the starlight that lit the night sky. Kwan and Gung Lao reminisced while they walked the path toward Koga Temple.

"Mistress, do you remember when I first came to Iga Temple? I couldn't have been older than eleven years old."

"Yes I remember. I was that age too. You always wanted to play with me and not the other boys."

"I remember it well. After…what happened to me, I became mistrustful around men."

"Do you mean…?"

Gung Lao cleared his throat, "I mean while I was enslaved… just look." He pulled his shirt up and revealed many whip lash scars. "My wretched master would whip me for no reason other than he felt the whim."

"Oh, spirits!" Kwan exclaimed.

"Ever since then I said I'd never harm anyone unless our lives were in danger. It's a promise I made with myself, and I intend to keep it."

"I'm a trained Iga ninja, Gung Lao. I will protect us," she reassured. Gung Lao smiled. Kwan did too.

They had run out of things to say so they went on in silence. It was not an awkward silence. No, it was a silence of mutually earnest comfort. Gung Lao had been there for Kwan through many hardships, and she for him. If she could trust anyone alive with her secrets, it was Gung Lao. That kind of trusting friendship was like the wind upon the waves.

"Gung Lao, is that…sobbing I hear from the brush?" she whispered. They paused and heard muffled tears.

"I hear it too. It sounds like a little girl. Should we check it out?"

"Yes of course, she could be in trouble." Hands on their weapons, Gung Lao parted the damp brush.

"I can't see over your shoulders. Who is it?" Kwan said in anticipation.

"It's a little girl. Oh, it's two little girls," he said. "I think I recognize one of them."

"Out of the way, you oaf," Kwan pressed him to the side and looked and saw them. One of them was kneeling and looked over her shoulder at them. The other slept, though appeared as if she was having unpleasant dreams.

"Miss Kwan?" the little girl said.

"Akari?! Akari-chan what are you doing here!" The two embraced.

"Miss Kwan! Miss Kwan! Thank the spirits it's you! Thank the spirits! Oh, I was so scared! I was so scared!" She squeezed Kwan even harder.

The other little girl stirred from her sleep and looked startled, keeping her arms close. "Akari, who're these people?"

"This is Miss Kwan. She is a ninja of Iga! We must have been close this whole time! Miss Kwan is the one that left me at Kyogama Town. Oh, I knew you would return one day, Miss Kwan. I knew it! Were you coming to get me? It was awful there, Miss Kwan. Awful."

The question took Kwan off guard. "I well…Not exactly Akari. You see, we're on a mission, me and Gung Lao here."

"Hello girls," Gung Lao said as he bowed. At least twice the height of either of them, the young girls were too intimidated to say anything in return. They merely gawked. But they looked at each other, then back to Gung Lao and bowed.

"Who is your little friend here, Akari?" Kwan said.

Mizu stood and stepped forward, "I'm Mizu. Akari-chan is my best friend."

"Nice to meet you Mizu-chan," Kwan said with a smile. "But what are you girls doing in the forest alone at night?"

The girls looked at each other again. Mizu began, "We ran away, Miss Kwan."

"The inn was awful," Akari said. "They had me wash dishes all day long. And when I was done with the dishes, they had me scrub the floors. And when I was done with the floors they had me take out garbage and chase rats. They were mean, Miss Kwan. Mean!"

"Well, I'm a little astonished. I had no idea they'd treat you like that Akari-chan." She looked at Gung Lao. "Let me and Gung Lao talk this over for a moment." Akari nodded.

The two adults stepped back out onto the path. "Gung Lao, Akari's parents were killed in the siege. Mother and father both."

"That makes her an orphan," Gung Lao replied. "Hm…should we take her back to the temple?"

"No, Iga Temple is almost a day's journey in the opposite direction. If we're to catch up with Iito, we can't take that kind of detour. And we can't just leave these two little girls alone in the woods."

"Hm...I wonder if Koga Temple could take them in. At least, for the time being. They're well known for accepting parentless children. And we're headed there anyway."

"Yes we're nearly there," she said. "Maybe an hour's walk away. But there's the matter of breaking the news of her parents to her...I don't have the heart to tell her. She's already so miserable."

"I think it best we tell someone at Koga Temple. Let her rest up and recover first. Then let them break the news," he said. Kwan thought it over for a moment and looked down the misty path toward Iga Temple as she bit her lip.

"Okay, let's bring them with us," she said. Gung Lao nodded as he led her back through the brush.

"Girls, we can't leave you two out here by yourselves. You must come with us to Koga Temple where it's safe."

"But Miss Kwan, we want to go to Iga Temple," Mizu said.

"That's where my mother and father live," Akari said. Kwan and Gung Lao looked at each other then back at Akari. Gung Lao gave her a very slight shake of the head as if to say *No, don't tell her.* Kwan caught the unspoken message.

"Akari-chan, it's late into the night and Koga Temple is very close. Iga Temple, on the other hand, is a day's walk."

"*A day's walk!*" Mizu exclaimed. "*You mean we passed it a day ago?!*"

"I told you I didn't know where it was!" Akari said.

"Regardless, you're coming with us to Koga. No more discussion."

"Anywhere's better than Kyogama Town," Mizu said to Akari.

"But, my mother," Akari said.

"We'll travel back there tomorrow after we get some rest," Mizu said. Akari had misgivings. She missed her mother deeply and missed her life as it once was. She used to spend hours a day gardening and arranging flowers in the courtyards of Iga Temple. Spending one more day away from her seemed intolerable. But maybe she could last just one more night.

"Okay Miss Kwan, we'll go with you," Akari said.

"Yes you will. Now let's get going."

"But Miss Kwan, where is that man you were with when last we met? The Koga ninja, I mean."

Kwan felt her heart sink. It struck her that Akari had not known about Unomichi's death. She grew weary and her feet beneath her became uneasy. Any reminder of his death nearly sent her into a spiral. Coming from someone as innocent as Akari, who had little experience with death, was doubly stressful. Having to explain death to children while talking about the one she grieved over would be too much. Luckily, Gung Lao was there to the rescue.

"Unomichi-san perished defending Iga Temple," he said. "That means he won't be around anymore." Even the soft language stung Kwan. Searching for answers had taken her mind off the pain of losing him. She was visibly upset. "Kwan are you alright?" he mumbled to her.

She wiped a tear from her eye. "I'm fine Gung Lao. Girls, we must go. Gather your things." The girls did as they were told and they stored their belongings into their packs. Gung Lao led the way out of the brush and the rest followed as they departed the camping spot down the path toward Koga Temple.

Chapter 11

Readings

"How long until we get to the channel?" Kasume asked. "It feels like we've been walking forever." Kasume walked with his hands clasped on the back of his head and his elbows stuck out.

"I already told you, Kasume," Hiriko replied, "We get there when we get there."

"It's already almost sundown. Maybe we could find somewhere to rest? Maybe a town or an inn? We've had to camp both nights we've been out," Kasume said. Hiriko started to chuckle. Puzzled, Kasume asked, "What's so funny?"

"Before we left, you said you love missions," Hiriko said. "And I said that you, without fail, always start to complain about them. Is complaining all you do, Kasume?"

Kasume tsked and hit his friend on the shoulder. "Shut up, Hiriko." The path curved up ahead, obscured by the trees rounding the corner. A few paces ahead of them, Riku sensed something. He motioned for them to stop.

"Someone's coming," Riku whispered. The three of them covered their ninjato handles and scurried to the inner side of the path. Hiriko and Kasume lined up behind Riku. The crunch of footsteps grew closer. "I hear a third footstep sound. Must be a walking stick. Maybe it's an elder," he whispered. They waited another moment and they began to hear light humming. It was an elderly man. He was white-haired and leaned on a polished wooden walking stick with a score around the top third. He bore a large knapsack strapped to his back. He seemed not to notice Riku and the others as he approached. But as he passed them on the path he paused and looked at them. He used his arm to wipe sweat off his brow.

"Care to hear a tale from an old traveling mystic?" he said in his aged voice. The ninjas relaxed and breathed sighs of relief. They took their hands off their sword hilts.

Riku replied, "Sorry sir, you frightened us. Why are you out on the path by yourself?"

He gave a smirk, "An old widower must earn a living somehow. Now, care for a story? It'll just cost you a coin."

Riku looked at the other two, who both shrugged as if to say, "Why not?"

"It couldn't hurt," Riku said. "Come, share a campfire with us."

"I must graciously refuse, young man, but I'll gladly tell my tale and be going." Riku dug in his pouch for a coin and presented it to the old mystic.

"Thank you." He joined them on the side of the path and they sat in a circle. They settled in and listened to him. Riku noticed the old man had a pungent smell, as if he hadn't bathed in weeks. A few moths fluttered nearby attracted to the smell.

The old mystic cleared his throat and began, "Many, many years ago, even before I was born, there was an ancient temple. The people of the temple lived happily under their lord, but the lord was himself unhappy. His wife had been missing for two years and most, including he, believed her to be dead. The people searched and searched for months but never found her. One day, she reappeared at the temple with a newborn child in her arms. Naturally the lord was conflicted. His beloved wife had reappeared, but she had borne someone else's child. He closed his heart to her and ordered the woman and child to be banished from the temple. She begged and moaned for him to accept them, but he refused. Exiled, the woman swore revenge on the lord and the temple. She groomed the boy to hate the temple and its lord, poisoning his soul, twisting it over and over until he became wicked and cruel."

Kasume intervened, "Ooh I think I've heard this before. Isn't this the fall of—" Hiriko elbowed Kasume in the chest.

"Let him tell the story!"

The old man continued. "The young man found he had a knack for persuasion. He gathered followers from the surrounding villages and together they trained to become warriors over a period of two years. When he felt they were ready, they launched an assault on the temple. The temple was unprepared and it fell within two days. The young man, now a war leader, went to the man that scorned him so long ago, the lord of the temple. Before the young war leader killed him, the lord put a terrible curse on him. He killed the lord and instead of taking over as its new leader, he ordered his men to burn the temple to the ground. The pain and hate in the man's heart did not fade after his victory and he lived the rest of his days in misery. He watched as his mother died and all his other loved ones slowly drifted away from him. Once he died, his hate and misery lived on and his spirit became a demon that still haunts the forests to this very day."

"Quite a sad story," Riku said.

"It's the story of the fall of Shō Temple," Kasume said. "I haven't heard it told like that before though. I had never heard of any curse placed on him. It usually ends right after the lord dies."

"Yes, yes. That detail is often neglected," the old man said. "But a very important detail it is. No one knows where the demon roams. Some say it remains at the Shō Temple ruins. Some say it roams from here to there sewing misfortune."

"I don't believe any of that nonsense," Hiriko said as he crossed his arms. Riku fingered his chin in contemplation. He had met demons in the human realm before. It was possible this demon could be real.

"Tell me mystic," Riku asked, "Do you read fortunes?"

The old man smirked. "But of course, young man. For another coin, of course." Riku dug into his pouch and handed him another coin, which the mystic stuffed into his own. "Okay now come close and show me your hands."

Riku scooched in front of the old man cross-legged and presented his hands. The mystic's hands were quite cold to the touch. He inspected Riku's palms closely, rubbing his fingers over different callouses and scars.

"I see, I see. You must be a warrior. Hm what else, what else…these creases here, they tell of much happiness in your future, but these…the folds here…they tell of sorrow. Horrible sorrow. Oh! Unbearable sorrow!" The mystic recoiled his hands.

"What kind of sorrow?" Riku pressed. *"What kind of sorrow? Tell me. Here, have another coin."* He dug into his pouch once again and handed him another coin and pressed it into his palm. The mystic looked at him with misgiving, but he took his hands once again.

"I see…an old acquaintance will cause you much grief." The mystic paused to try to tell more. "That's all I can read. But the future is not set in stone. It never is. Much can be changed. Much, much can be changed, yes."

Riku sat back and mulled over what the mystic said. *An old acquaintance will cause me much grief. But who could that be? Will Zeshiro return to haunt me once again? I had hoped giving him Dragon Fang would appease him. And what of this demon lord he insisted needed to be stopped? Too many unanswered questions.*

"Ooh ominous," Kasume joked.

"Yeah I don't believe any of this future-telling nonsense either," Hiriko inserted. The old mystic furled his brow and seemed displeased. "S-sorry sir. It's just that I believe that we design our own destiny. You said it yourself that nothing is set in stone."

"Indeed," he replied. "But destiny has a way of working itself out one way or another. Free will is a gift given to us from the heavens, but our free will is merely a vehicle through which we carry out the will of the spirits. So, it is free will we have, yet it is also predetermined, if that makes any sense to you."

"Kind of," Kasume said as he scratched his head.

"When will this acquaintance cause me this grief?" Riku asked. The old mystic stood up and dusted himself off.

"That is only for the spirits to know. I only see mere shadows of the future, not clear-cut images. But, alas, I must be going." He stood, collected himself, and gave a bow.

"Thank you, sir," they said in turn. They stood up and bowed to him. He started down the path and resumed his hums as the gravel crunched beneath his feet. The moths followed him as he left as if drawn to his stench. The three of them listened until the crunching footsteps faded away.

Kasume broke the silence, "That guy gave me the creeps." The three of them returned to their spots on the ground and knelt in comfortable positions.

Hiriko chimed in, "He seemed friendly enough, but he seemed to have a negative aura around him. He smelled awful."

"I felt it too," Riku said. "We must stay on guard. We can never know what is around the corner." Riku felt cold steel press against his neck.

"Riku," the sweet voice of a woman whispered. "I knew I'd find you eventually." All color left Riku's face as he hesitated to make a movement. He could not so much as turn his head to see who it was.

"A shadow!" Kasume gasped. He readied his ninjato. Hiriko took his bow off his shoulder and readied an arrow. It was an ephemeral shadow that held a ninjato to Riku's throat from behind. The sun had gone down but the shadow was darker even than the surrounding darkness. Riku could see it out of the corner of his eye and slowly inched his right hand across his hip to his own ninjato. When he finally reached it, in one swift motion he stood up and knocked the blade away from his throat. He stabbed into the darkness. The sword struck true. The intruder did not so much as whimper. A woman fell out of the shadow onto the ground. To his dismay he recognized the woman in her sapphire kimono immediately. The kimono was in tatters and had mud and blood stains all over it with thorns and needles caught in the fabric.

"*Yuuki-chan!*" Riku cried. He bent down to hold her. Yuuki had an awful stench like she had been dead for weeks. He shook her but she was lifeless and cold.

"Yuuki-chan. Oh, my Yuuki-chan. What's happened to you? Spirits above, why?" The shadow Yuuki had fallen out of still lingered, but Riku was too distraught to care. He held her lifeless body to his chest and began to weep.

Kasume and Hiriko remained on guard. Their eyes darted between the distraught ninja and the ephemeral shadow.

A mysterious voice from within the shadow said, "Riku-san, I've found you at last." Riku looked over his shoulder as another woman he recognized stepped out of the darkness.

"Chi?" Riku stuttered, hardly able to talk over his tears. "What are you doing here?" Unomichi's estranged wife Chi was dressed in an emerald kimono. Her hair was done up as if she had just left a formal occasion. She revealed a strap attached to her leg that held a knife.

"I've been looking for you, Riku. My dark master is asking for your head." She pulled out the knife and made a move toward him. He let go of Yuuki's body and rolled out of the way. Hiriko swooped in with his sword to block her downward blow.

"Out of the way, boy," she spat. "This does not concern you."

Riku picked himself up and was shocked at the circumstances. "Chi, what have you done to Yuuki?"

"I did as my master commanded. I tortured her slowly. Oh! Did she bleed and bleed. She begged for me to kill her."

Still reeling from the shock, Riku asked, "Chi what has come over you? Who is this dark master you speak of?"

Chi gave a menacing giggle. "He's a demon lord. He is cunning and cruel, incredibly powerful, ancient, primordial, a force of nature. He intends to take control of the human realm, and it *will* happen. It is inevitable. If you stand in his way, you either join him, or you die. It's that simple."

"You joined with a demon lord? You'd betray us all?! Unacceptable!" Riku said.

"You don't understand, Riku. He's been planning his invasion for years. Our fate is written. We must join him or die. Will you join me in serving him?"

"Chi, we are not going to join with a demon lord. That's total madness!"

She smirked. "He said you would refuse. I'm forced to dispatch you myself then." She held the dagger with her left hand, reached back with her right and shoved her palm toward him. The energy pulse knocked Riku off his feet. She swung around and sent another blast, then another, each one pushed him back tumbling. Kasume threw a kunai at her but she sent a blast at the dagger which deflected it out of the way and knocked

Kasume off his feet. Hiriko shot an arrow at her, but she gusted it aside and knocked him back too.

"We can't get close to her!" Kasume called. With a crazed look on her face, she sent blast after blast at them and forced them across the path. The blasts brought sharp gravel and debris with them. She began to laugh as she sent more and more energy pulses. Riku and the others could not keep their footing. A white-hooded figure that wore a golden mask stepped out of the shadow behind Chi. He held a sword that glowed with a purple luster. Soon, another figure made of stone that wore white samurai armor and carried a white-bladed sword over his shoulder approached from out of the shadow as well.

The hooded figure spoke, "Do I always have to intervene for you Riku?"

"Zeshiro! Aurabos!" Kasume called as he struggled just to stand.

"You appear to be in danger," the stone demon said.

"A little help, you two," Riku cried. Chi looked over her shoulder at the demons.

"Zeshiro, what are you doing here?" she asked incredulously. "And how did you acquire Dragon Fang?"

Zeshiro slowly walked toward her as he held the violet-glowing silver sword in front of him. "Riku lent it to me. I owe him for it. I'll have to defend him."

"You're with *him*? So, it *is* true. Our dark lord will have your head for betraying him!"

"I mean to destroy him. Some things are more important than my own head."

"*You treacherous cur.* I'll bring him your head myself!" She reeled her hand back and sent an energy pulse at him. Without breaking pace, Zeshiro took heavy step after heavy step towards her as he held Dragon Fang in front of him. It split the energy pulse in half. Aurabos and the others watched.

Chi sent another blast, again split in two by Dragon Fang. She began to back up. She futilely sent more and more blasts as Zeshiro stoically drew closer and closer. And when he was within a pace, he lunged forward and stabbed her through the stomach with the legendary sword.

Zeshiro spoke as he pulled out the glowing sword and the woman fell to her knees, "Little girls shouldn't meddle with dark magic." He flicked her blood off the legendary sword.

"He is coming, Zeshiro," she coughed as blood dripped from her mouth. "The demon lord is coming." She slumped over lifeless.

"The demon lord is already here," Zeshiro said as Riku and the others got up and dusted off the debris. "He wanders about the forest, festering evil energy wherever he travels. Be wary of travelers crossing your path."

Riku asked, "How fares Dragon Fang? There are many times I've felt conflicted over my decision to hand it over to you."

"As you can see, it's in proper form," Zeshiro said. "And it has already proven to be a good decision on your part."

Aurabos chimed in, "I have ensured the safety of Dragon Fang myself. Both the sword and its wielder."

"Very good," Riku said. He bowed to the imposing stone demon.

"Your wife though…" Zeshiro stepped next to the corpse of Riku's deceased wife. He lifted her arm and felt its limp coldness. "She must have been dead for weeks. We witnessed that wretched Chi drag her lifeless body through Onigawa. We followed her here."

"The dark lord must have had her killed. He seems to have something against you personally, Riku. Perhaps he knew you would wield Dragon Fang. That woman, Chi. You knew her?"

Riku responded, "She was married to my brother-in-arms Unomichi." He rubbed his chin. "Come to think of it, she came to Koga Temple one day and quickly became betrothed to Unomichi."

"She must have been a spy of the demon lord. She probably told him everything there is to know about you."

"But they were married for years," Riku protested. "They had a son together and everything."

Zeshiro thought it over for a moment then said, "The demon lord is very old and has great patience. He has spies lurking everywhere. Some, such as her, are in deep cover."

Aside, Kasume asked his friend, "Hiriko, are you a demon spy?"

Hiriko slugged him in the chest, "Shut up, Kasume."

Zeshiro continued, "We've been tracking the demon lord in and out of *Onigawa*.

"What have you learned?" Riku asked.

"He seems to have returned to the human realm once again. He's a master of disguise and can appear in any number of forms."

"Shapeless…like water." Riku pondered. "How do we defeat such an enemy?"

"This right here," Zeshiro said as he tapped his palm with the broad side of Dragon Fang. Aurabos' eyes tightened.

"Tell me Riku," Aurabos began, "what has become of the legendary sword Tiger Claw? Its safety is of my concern."

Riku rubbed the back of his neck. "The last I heard of it, it's in the possession of the Iga ninja Kwan. You remember her, yes?"

"Ah yes, Kwan. Of course I remember her."

"I'm sure it's in good hands," Riku assured. Riku looked over at the body of his former wife as it rested on the grass next to the path. "I'm not sure what to do next. I can't leave my wife's body here. But I need to complete my mission." Zeshiro and Aurabos looked at each other.

Zeshiro asserted, "We will take her body from here. We can bring her with us back to Koga Temple. For us, it is only a slight detour."

"I would appreciate it greatly, Zeshiro." Riku said distraught. "Yuuki-chan deserves to rest in peace. When I return, I will pay her my proper respects." He looked at her longingly, tears developing in his eyes.

"Think nothing of it," Zeshiro said. "Her body is safe with us. You should focus on your mission." Riku looked down and away.

"There is…one more thing Zeshiro. My mission could prove fruitful in helping with the demon lord. I can't get into specifics, or even confirm that this is true, but I may be able to contribute."

106

"We can use every bit of help we can get," Zeshiro said. "Let's go, Aura."

"Right," the stone demon said. He stabbed the wind sword into the ground, reached and picked up Yuuki's body. He placed her over his shoulder before he recovered his sword. "We'll make sure she gets a proper burial," he assured.

"Thank you Aura. Zeshiro."

The demons nodded and carried the body with them down the path toward Koga Temple. They were gone. Riku sniffled and tried to muffle the sounds of his pain. Hiriko and Kasume came to comfort him. Riku tightened his fists.

The demon lord must be stopped. He did this to Yuuki. I'll do the same to him. But wait. The scroll from Hokkenzen Shrine. Instead of bringing back Unomichi, I could instead use it to…no…no it wouldn't be right.

Chapter 12

Ogoshi

Kwan and Gung Lao were each given a guest bedroom once they arrived at Koga Temple late at night. Akari and Mizu insisted they be given a shared bedroom for themselves. All three rooms were essentially the same: tatami flooring, a thickly padded bedroll for each guest, and sliding shoji doors common in the temple. Akari particularly enjoyed the open-air window with a sliding fusuma shutter.

Kwan tossed and turned all night. Nightmares of the attack and of the ephemeral dragon in its violet majesty that burned Unomichi to ash haunted her all night. Several times she had to sit up over the side of her bed and remember that it was all in the past. Then she would collapse back onto the bed and struggle to fall back asleep, just to experience the same nightmare again.

Morning came and she did not feel rested at all. Gung Lao in the next room had slept soundly and, full of energy, came into her room to check on her.

"How are the girls?" Kwan asked him.

"They are still asleep in the next room over." Thuds and the sound of little girls running around proved him wrong. Kwan threw her blankets over and all but tripped over herself to reproach them in their room.

She entered and noticed it was in disarray with blankets and pillows thrown sloppily all over the floor. "Girls, you must show respect to the temple! People are still trying to sleep! The sun is barely up!"

They fell silent as if caught red-handed. Mizu said, "Sorry Miss Kwan. We were just excited to be here at the temple. I never thought I'd ever come to a place like this."

"Very well, but still, keep it down! We're going to speak with the Grandmaster of the temple this afternoon." Akari and Mizu gasped and looked at each other. Kwan continued, "Now get yourselves cleaned up and ready. You want to make a good first impression."

"Okay Miss Kwan," Akari bowed.

An hour later Akari and Mizu emerged from their shared room. They asked a servant for kimonos with flower print and they brought them a pink one and a pale green one, both with the print they asked for. Mizu put Akari's dark hair in a braid how she liked it and Akari tied Mizu's dark hair in two pig tails.

At this time in the late morning, the young ninjas practiced their forms in the training grounds of the courtyard. Kwan and Gung Lao took the girls for a stroll around the open-air interior of the temple. She wore her black kimono with flower print and Gung Lao wore black robes typical of Koga Temple. The two adults strolled through the gardens and the young girls followed. The leaves of the cherry blossom trees were vibrant reds and yellows. A pond of still water rippled after a red leaf broke away and fell to the surface. The aroma of fresh autumn air that blew through her hair reminded Kwan of years ago when she would

109

camp deep in the forest with her friends when she was younger and still a kunoichi in training. They were out for many days in a row to learn advanced survival techniques like how to catch wild animals, how to follow tracks, and how to start campfires only using things in found nature. It was that kind of pleasant memory she thought about when times were tough.

Off in the distance they could hear the *kyah*'s and *osu*'s of the Koga ninjutsu practitioners. After they made their way through the gardens, they approached the side of the training area, though they were careful not to step on the hallowed ground. It was hewn of stone in contrast to the lushness of the natural gardens elsewhere in the courtyard. As they passed by, they turned their heads and watched the form routines of the ninjas. Kwan noticed that their style was different from that of Iga Temple. It seemed the Koga style consisted of frequent misdirection compared to Iga's style of straight forwardness. She had seen the Koga style before in real battle during the attack and it seemed highly effective. The Koga ninja would feint an attack high, then strike low, or feint left and attack right. One never knew what to expect when fighting them.

While they stared at the practitioners, none of them noticed the man in white ceremonial robes that stood at the corner they approached. "Kwan-san, how good of you to join us," Grandmaster Minato hailed as he cordially bowed. The group paused and faced him before they did the same.

"Grandmaster Minato," Kwan said.

He smiled. "Who are these little ones you've brought with you, Kwan-san?" She motioned to Akari and Mizu who could not tear their eyes away from their feet. The ninjutsu practitioners in the square took no notice and continued their exercises, giving off the occasional *kyah*.

"Their names are Akari and Mizu. I met Akari while Iga Temple was under siege. Her and her friend Mizu here were escaping an…unacceptable housing arrangement in Kyogama Town."

"I see," Minato said as he glanced down at the young girls. Akari stole a look at the Grandmaster, and then another before she returned her eyes to the ground below while Mizu kept her eyes locked on her own feet. "Very respectful, you seem to be."

Kwan interjected, "Grandmaster, the girls lack anyone to guide them." She looked down at the girls in front of her, not wanting to give Akari the grim news of the fate of her parents. "Grandmaster…can I speak with you alone?"

He responded with a questioning look, but it faded in an instant. "Of course, Kwan-san. Come."

"Thank you, Grandmaster. Gung Lao, watch the girls for a moment."

"Yes, Mistress," Gung Lao replied. "Come girls, let's watch the ninjas practice." He shuffled them to turn around and Akari locked eyes with Kwan before she turned her back.

Kwan could not think of a delicate way to tell him what she had to say. "Grandmaster Minato-sama, I gathered the girls with me because I knew they have not a single guardian between them to look after them. Mizu's parents are long dead and Akari's parents both perished in the siege. I have my own mission to carry out and well…"

Minato's voice gave a knowing grumble. "I see where this is going. You'd like us to take them in here at Koga Temple."

Kwan felt a sack full of potatoes worth of weight fall off her shoulders. "Minato-sama, you always seem able to read my mind. Yes, can I leave them here?" Minato went quiet while he thought over their predicament. After a silence so dense one could slice through it, he said, "We don't allow freeloaders to persist off our temple. If they are to stay here they must be a boon to us." Kwan tightened her jaw and looked down. What could the girls possibly offer the temple? "You appear not to see what is in plain sight, Kwan-san. Akari and Mizu would make excellent ninjas under my tutelage." Kwan's face lit up. "I can sense their energy. A very bright future is ahead of them here at Koga. If they wish it."

"But her mother and father—"

"She will learn of it in due time."

Gung Lao watched the ninjutsu practitioners toss their partners onto the ground. He held Mizu's hand on his left and Akari's on his right. Mizu was dazzled by the display and commonly pointed at the ninjas' throws. Akari tried to watch but she could not help but glance over at Kwan and Minato deep in discussion.

"Did you see that Gung Lao?!" Mizu cheered. "She tossed him flat on his back!" Gung Lao chuckled. "Look at that! Boom pow ow! That looked like it hurt! Wow! Over there! He flipped him over!" Mizu jumped up and down and cheered. "Gung Lao did you see that?!"

"I saw it, Mizu-chan, I saw it!" Gung Lao said. "That throw is called *ogoshi* or 'big hip throw.' I like to practice it too!"

"Ooh can you show me? Can you show me?"

"They're doing it right now!" he pointed. "Watch them." One of the ninjas grabbed his partner's wrist, put his other arm around the waist, squared his hips in front of his partner's, and in one motion lifted him up onto his back and tossed him over. Mizu cheered. Akari's eyes watched the ninjas, but her ears were focused on Kwan's conversation. Kwan looked over her shoulder at them.

"Akari! Mizu! Come here!" Kwan called. "Grandmaster Minato has a proposition for you both." The girls looked at each other, then scurried over to her, leaving Gung Lao in the dust. He followed with his heavy steps after them. When they were all settled, Akari and Mizu stood side by side and faced Kwan and the Grandmaster.

He began, "Girls, have you ever considered what will become of you in the future?" The girls glanced at each other and raised their palms before they returned to attention. "Hmm. Like young lotus buds ready to bloom in the nurturance of the sunlight of early spring, you two will one day blossom into young women with all the freedom and responsibility that come with it. Without proper care, you could become wild and reckless, heedless to any authority, and will more than likely succumb to your own carelessness. However, I offer you this: If you wish it, I will allow you to reside here and train to become Koga kunoichi." Mizu's face lit up and she bounced up and down. She hugged her friend. Akari was slack-jawed. Her eyes went wide and peered at Minato.

Kwan cut in, "Now girls, it takes a great deal of discipline to train to become a ninja. Lots of hard work and dedication is required. It will take years."

Without thinking about it, Mizu chimed in, "*Hai!* I accept, Grandmaster!" Akari looked at her with a blank face.

Akari began, "But what would my mother say?" A moment passed before the silence was broken.

Minato said firmly, yet delicately, "She would no doubt be proud to have a daughter that grew to become a Koga ninja."

Akari looked up at Kwan who gave an encouraging smile and nod. Akari said, "If Miss Kwan says I can, then I will." They all looked at Kwan.

Suddenly on the spot, Kwan gathered herself and said, "I can't make that decision for you. You must make it for yourself. But if you're looking for my permission, then I consent."

Akari looked from Kwan to Grandmaster Minato. "Ok, I agree," she muffled.

"I didn't hear you," Minato said.

Akari squeezed her fists and shouted, more to convince herself than anyone else, "*Hai!* I will become a great Koga kunoichi!"

"Very good," Minato accepted and bowed. He looked from one to the other. "You are both fortunate to have an adequate training partner. I look forward to watching you grow strong and formidable. We will begin your training once you get your proper uniforms."

Kwan turned to Minato, "Grandmaster, there is more I wish to discuss with you. In private."

"Alright then, let's head to my office quarters." He motioned to his servant. "Mikoto, prepare the tea."

Chapter 13

No More Tears

The tea in her porcelain teacup was piping hot and it stung Kwan's lips at the merest taste. The beautiful servant Mikoto wore white silk robes. She bowed as she slid open the fusuma and exited the room. She slid it closed behind her. Minato, who sat behind the low oak table, could not take his eyes off her until she left the room. The late morning sunlight that struck the shaded walls brightened the otherwise murky office. The black ink of the monochrome ukiyo-e prints of serpentine dragons and mountains emboldened when the light streamed through them. Kwan blew on her tea and remained silent, unsure of how to present her question. Grandmaster Minato remained silent as well. He sat cross-legged with his eyes closed while the fragrant aroma of the herbal tea made its way to his nose.

He began, "Nothing pleases me these days quite like a pleasant cup of tea. Don't you agree?"

"Er…I…yes, Grandmaster," she replied.

"Mmm. I often reflect on the notes of the seasonal blends. The flakes of leaves on the tail-end of their prime alter the taste in savory ways. Autumn teas always remind me of the passing of time, the constancy of change. The only certainty of life is impermanence. But therein lies beauty. When one studies a blossoming lotus, it is the will of the universe that that particular view is both a once-ever and never-again phenomenon."

"But what of the things we wish to keep forever? Are they not also beautiful?"

"They are beautiful as well, yes. But remember, all things change. The things we desire most are most desirable because they are so fleeting. And the things we expect to always rely on, once taken away, are missed the most. But such is the way of the universe and the passage of time."

Kwan soaked in his words with a long draft of tea. "Unomichi's passing…I don't know if I can ever let it go," she said. "My thoughts are on it during the day. When I sleep, I have nightmares. The flames, the purple fire, the ashes. I relive it every night. One moment he was there, the next he was not. The loss I feel—"

"It will pass, Kwan-san. It will pass with time." Minato took a long sniff of his tea before taking a sip.

"You seem almost dismissive, Grandmaster. His killer walks alive and free while I am left here in shambles. Surely Riku will be held accountable. Where is he?"

"I understand your pain, young ninja. I understand. But I sent him away on a mission and he cannot be interfered with at this time." Kwan lost herself and let a fierce grimace overtake her countenance.

"That's not good enough, Grandmaster!" Tiger Claw, attached to her hip, vibrated as if it sensed her emotion. "Riku must be brought to justice!" she said sharply. "If you do not comply, I will do it myself." Minato's eyes widened. "Now *where is he?"* She unconsciously let her hand cover the handle of her sword. Her heart beat so hard it felt as if it would burst out of her chest.

"Control yourself, Kwan! I will not tolerate ferocious demands in my office! Not after Iito just came through himself! It seems everyone is looking for Riku since I sent him away!"

Kwan took a deep breath and collected herself. Once calmed, she said, "Grandmaster…where did you send him? This is important to me."

Minato considered for a moment and took a sip of tea. "I sent him to Hokkenzen Shrine on the island to the north, Hokkaido."

Kwan felt her stomach drop. She had heard of Hokkenzen Shrine before. It was at the peak of a frigid, inhospitable mountain. "Now, *why* would you send him to such a remote shrine? He should have been brought to justice! Not sent to some far-off location!"

Unshaken, Minato took a calculatedly long draft of his tea. "The *why* is between me and Riku. Though, it appears that Riku's mission will directly benefit you. But beyond that, I can tell you no more. You must learn to control your emotions Kwan-san, or, in the heat of battle, you may find yourself under their control. Master your emotions, or they will master *you.*"

"I've had enough of your secrets, Grandmaster! And I don't understand why you will not cooperate or see things how I see them!"

Another deep sip. "Reflect on what I just told you. Also, consider my perspective on the matter. It is because of Riku's actions that this temple still stands. If I were to gravely punish him, there would be an uprising demanding my head. Now, I've answered your questions. You should gather your things and leave the temple by day's end. If you want to confront Riku, I will not stand in your way, but it will be at your own peril."

Rather than face any more denials of her wishes, Kwan placed her teacup back onto the table with enough force that it splashed and spilled. She sprang to her feet, clenched her teeth, and took her leave. Minato allowed himself a shrug before taking another sip from his teacup. To himself he said, "What a poor waste of good tea." He reached over and slid her teacup in front of himself.

Kwan, dejected, stormed down the path along the padded flooring of the indoor training area. She saw Gung Lao and the girls still watching the martial arts practice from the corner of the training grounds. Gung Lao turned his head and noticed her at once. She tried to hide the irritation scored onto her face. While she took her hurried strides toward them, Gung Lao asserted, "I assume it did not go well."

With tightened lips she said, "We have a new destination. Hokkenzen Shrine."

"Hokkenzen Shrine!" he exclaimed. "But that's across—"

"I know."

"And atop—"

"*I know!* But that's where Riku is headed. I imagine he is taking his time. If we hurry, there's a possibility we catch him before he crosses the channel." Gung Lao sighed. Kwan decided against letting him know how badly she botched the conversation with Grandmaster Minato. Some details were better left unsaid.

Akari spoke up. "You're leaving already? But we just got here!"

Kwan looked down at the young girl. "The Koga will look after you from now on."

"My mother…" Akari mumbled. "She's dead, isn't she…?" Kwan crouched to meet Akari at eye level and she put her hands on the little girl's shoulders to comfort her.

Kwan quickly forgot her indignation. "I'm so sorry, Akari-chan," Kwan said. "She died like so many others during the attack on Iga Temple." The two embraced. Akari had suspected it and had already accepted it, though she prayed she was wrong. While she toiled away for a month, scrubbed Spirits-knew how many dishes, and had not received a single word from home, she lost hope of ever seeing her mother again. It was almost a relief that she knew the truth, as sad a truth as it was. She let out only one whimper and sobbed silently onto Kwan's shoulder as she squeezed hard.

"I wasn't there. I wasn't strong enough. I just ran away," Akari said.

Kwan asked, "What could you have done against them?"

Akari said nothing. *Weak…I was too weak and afraid. It was those cursed demons. Never again. Never.* She looked over at Mizu whose eyebrows were tightened in concern. Mizu rushed to her and gave her a hug.

"You'll always have me, Akari," Mizu said. She could feel Akari's tears on her own shoulder. "I'll be right there beside you.

Best friends forever. It's a promise." Tears gathered in her own eyes.

When the girls were done with their embrace, Kwan said, "Girls, Grandmaster Minato and the Koga will look after you from now on. Gung Lao and I must continue with our mission. I expect you both to be on your best behavior. I don't want to hear that you've been goofing off. When I come back you'll show me all you've learned. Mizu-chan, stay by Akari's side. This is a difficult time for her. She needs a good friend. She needs you."

"Yes, of course Miss Kwan," Mizu said.

"Gung Lao, we must prepare and leave by day's end," Kwan said.

"Yes Mistress," Gung Lao replied. "It's awfully cold at Hokkenzen Shrine."

Akari sank to the ground as the adults walked to their quarters. The ninjas continued their practice. She looked at her palms as she cried. Mizu rubbed her back. Akari sulked, "Mother. My mother…"

"It's okay to cry Akari-chan. When I learned my parents were…gone…I cried too. A lot."

"I'm tired of crying, Mizu. I have no more tears." She got up and Mizu did too shortly after. "Let's train hard. Let's become strong. For our mothers."

"For our mothers," Mizu said, "and for us."

"And for us." Akari wiped away the last of her tears. "I was too weak. I should've been strong and fought that demon that day. But instead, I ran. I ran like a little child."

121

"Akari, you *are* a child. You didn't kill your mother. It was the demons."

Akari looked down and to the side for a moment, then looked into Mizu's eyes. "Now that I'm here, I will become the strongest kunoichi the Koga have ever known. *And I'll kill every demon I ever meet.*" She was convinced.

"And I'll be right there beside you." Mizu presented her hand between them and Akari grasped it.

/ / /

A female servant in white robes and dark hair slid open the fusuma of the bedroom Akari and Mizu shared. The girls looked up. "Girls, I brought your training uniforms as requested by Grandmaster Minato." She placed a black martial arts uniform and a white belt before each of them. A man appeared at the door whom Akari recognized as one of the men that trained in the courtyard.

"Girls, my name is Daisuke." He bowed, and they scrambled to their feet and did the same. "I will be your chief ninjutsu instructor here at the temple. If you have any questions, direct them to me. Or to Grandmaster Minato of course."

"When do we begin training?" Akari pressed.

Taken aback by her enthusiasm Daisuke blinked. He quickly composed himself. "Eager? Your training will start tomorrow just before sunrise. Wear those uniforms. It is said that everyone is born with a white belt. As such, that is where you'll begin."

Chapter 14

By Starlight

The sun rested on the horizon as Kwan and Gung Lao departed from Koga Temple. "Riku is a few days ahead of us, Gung Lao. If we hurry, maybe we can catch up to him before he crosses the channel," Kwan said.

"I'd say it's worth the attempt," Gung Lao replied. "I'd rather not freeze my ears off on the northern island if I could help it."

"Let's make haste then," she said. Under her black robes with flower print she wore thicker, white cotton robes. She had to be prepared for the harsh cold of the mountains if it came to it. Tiger Claw clung to her hip in its sheath. It gave off a slight warmth, just barely noticeable against her leg. Gung Lao wore a moss-colored cotton coat and a matching cotton hat with trousers. He wore his short sword against his hip, a less fancy blade than Tiger Claw, but serviceable enough.

The pair headed northeast along the packed gravel road. The forest was dense on both sides, with clearings here and there along the way. They trotted along at a brisk pace. Kwan remembered running long distances without stopping as part of her Iga ninja training. Though untrained as a ninja, Gung Lao had become as fit as possible to best protect his closest companion Kwan if it ever came to it. After an hour of running, the sun had completely hidden beneath the horizon and only starlight lit their way. "We must keep moving, Gung Lao," she panted. "We need to catch up with him before it's too late." The pale white stones of the path were visible enough in the darkness for them to keep running. She felt the air grow colder as the night wore on, the autumn breeze blew loose dead leaves and grasses across the path. It chilled their faces and they shuddered, but they continued to run.

"Mistress, let us rest for a spell at the next clearing," Gung Lao panted. Kwan considered for a moment and then agreed. Before long they came upon a clearing on the northern side of the path. As they approached they could see a campfire with an elderly woman sitting alone gazing into it. As they approached, colorful butterflies flapped and fluttered as they swirled in the wind near the fire.

"Come closer young ones. Come closer," the elderly woman beckoned them. She sat on a felled tree trunk that faced the makeshift fire. She was old, Kwan guessed in her late seventies or eighties, and hunched. She gave off a pleasant smell. Her gray hair was shriveled but kept as clean as she could manage. "There is a beautiful view of the stars from here," the old woman said. It was customary to treat fellow travelers kindly. Nevertheless, they approached hesitantly. "Come, come. Rest by the fire."

"Thank you ma'am," Gung Lao said as he bowed.

"Thank you," Kwan relented. They took their seats next to each other on the tree trunk opposite the fire from her. Kwan looked up at the butterflies as they circulated a little quicker above the fire.

"You know," the old woman said, "the Spirits in the stars are looking down upon us, watching after us, judging us." She pointed to the stars through the foliage. "Do you see that constellation there?" She pointed to stars that made an x formation. "That is the mighty Falcon that sees all. He is a fierce protector of the righteous. Oh, and who could forget that group there? That crystalline pattern is that of the Icy Bear in its slumber. And do you see that grouping of eight stars? That is the constellation of the Great Tigress. Beautiful and powerful, isn't she? She is ever hunting the Spirit Dragon, those nine stars over there. See how the stars zigzag? The Spirit Dragon stole the lover of the Great Tigress, so the Tigress eternally chases the Dragon across the sky."

Kwan absorbed the story and something about it made her heart beat faster. Gung Lao was growing sleepy and he was so preoccupied with how tired he was that he failed to listen to the old woman. "Does the Great Tigress ever catch the Spirit Dragon? Does she ever get her revenge?" Kwan asked.

The old woman cleared her throat. "One day she will. One day."

"And what happens then? What happens when the Dragon is caught?" Kwan pressured.

The old woman was silent for a moment and looked into Kwan's eyes from across the fiery wisps. "The light of the Tigress's stars will quench. Her mission complete, she will shift into the Great Beyond." Gung Lao took slow heavy breaths as

126

he began to fall asleep where he sat. Kwan hit him on the arm and he snorted awake. "At least, that's what the stories say. Now, what are a young couple such as yourselves doing on the road at this hour?"

"Oh, we're not—" Kwan stuttered.

"I'm...we're...not together ma'am," Gung Lao asserted. "I'm her servant. We're from Iga Temple. On a mission."

"Oh, I see. Traveling companions then." The old woman chuckled. Kwan blushed and Gung Lao scratched the back of his neck. "I suppose you couldn't tell an old woman what your mission is about?"

"We couldn't tell you. It would put you in harm's way. Someone could try to threaten you for the information. Better if you didn't know," Kwan said.

"Oh, no one would threaten an old woman," she said.

Kwan scrunched up her mouth and decided the old woman was right. What was the harm in telling her? "We're chasing after someone. This man is going to Hokkenzen Shrine."

"Ah yes, Hokkenzen Shrine," she recalled. "I wonder if he's going there to resurrect someone, perhaps a loved one?"

"What did you say?" Kwan asked.

"People only go to Hokkenzen Shrine to pray to bring someone back to life. Perhaps he's lost someone special to him."

Gung Lao chimed in, "I heard his wife had gone missing and is likely dead."

Kwan felt a surge of emotion rush through her. *Unomichi! I could travel there to bring back Unomichi!* She breathed heavily.

127

"Mmm," the old woman grumbled, "but it is said the prayer only works once every hundred years. After that, the spirits will remain silent for all others until the next opportunity."

All the energy Kwan felt rush through her condensed into a steel ball that sank into her stomach. *Riku is going to use the spell to bring back his wife. There is no way he wouldn't. Unless I get there first. And when I meet him there, I'll make him pay.* Tiger Claw rumbled in its sheath.

The fire flickered as it tried to hold onto its existence despite the wind. Gung Lao looked over his shoulder into the dark forest around them. He thought he heard a twig snapping underfoot but decided to keep it to himself. The vegetation rustled wildly in the wind sending a shiver through their coats, though, Kwan felt none the colder since Tiger Claw kept her warm.

She felt her eyelids growing heavy as she gazed into the fire. Running all evening made her back sore and her legs ache. She nearly fell off the log as she felt wakefulness leave her. Gung Lao caught her with his arm around her back, after which she jolted awake.

"Let us spend the night here at the campfire, Mistress," Gung Lao pleaded. "We'll make much more progress when we're fully rested."

Gung Lao took out their bedrolls from within their packs and spread them out next to the fire. As Kwan laid down, her back to the fire, she cradled Tiger Claw between her arms. It was not long before she descended into deep sleep. Gung Lao laid down next to her. The old woman alternated between watching them and gazing into the fire.

/ / /

The frigid air burned Kwan's skin. Her robes offered very little protection against the cold. Every breeze felt like a dry, icy bath. She might have frozen to death had Tiger Claw's aura not warmed her. The silver sword gave an orange gleam, the claw marks on its blade near the base glowed brightest of all. She held it firmly in front of her, her right foot slightly in front of her left. Across the icy stretch was her lover, Unomichi, his own sword in hand, though there was something off about him.

"I've travelled across the world to find you," Kwan pleaded. She wanted to run to him. To hold him and kiss him again as they once did. But she found herself unable to move. "I ran for miles. I crossed the channel. I climbed this frozen mountain. For you. To find you so we could be together again. Why will you not listen? *Why will you not listen to me?*"

"The man you knew as Unomichi is dead," the man said as his eyes narrowed. "You killed him. It was your fault. Your fault."

"No! It was not me! *It was not me!*" she pleaded. She wanted to fall to her knees. Tears welled up in her eyes, tears that grew colder as they trailed down her face.

"If not you, then who?" he spat.

"...Riku. It was Riku," she whispered.

"Then kill him. Kill Riku. Kill Riku. Kill Riku." Unomichi's face contorted until it became that of Riku's.

"Yahhh!!" She ran at him, bringing Tiger Claw above her head. The snowy air she rushed through grew colder as she

129

closed the distance. Just before she brought the blade down with a mighty stroke, she woke up.

/ / /

She gasped for breath. Kwan sat up and saw Gung Lao fast asleep on his side. The fire had gone out. "Gung Lao, wake up. Wake up." She nudged him.

"Five more minutes Mistress. Five more minutes."

Despite her companion being too groggy to perceive what she said, she wanted to speak anyway. "I had another nightmare. But this one was different. I've never had before."

"A different nightmare?" he said half-awake, voice still hoarse. He gave a sigh. "Pay it no heed. It's just a dream, nothing more." He rolled his big shoulders onto his back.

"Where's the old woman we met last night? There's no sign of her," Kwan asked.

"She must've left sometime this morning. Early too." He rubbed the sleep out of his eyes and saw the pinks and oranges of the sunrise to the east across the path.

"That woman was strange. There was something odd about her. I can't quite put my finger on it," she said.

"Yes, I agree. And what was she doing traveling by herself at night? I never got a chance to ask her."

"How peculiar."

The chill of the morning began to soften as the rising sun warmed the autumn air. Only a few clouds floated in the sky above though it was still quite chilly. The morning forest smelled of a mix of sweet pine and maple. The last of the golden and coral leaves still clung to the trees' extensions.

Kwan jumped to her feet. "We need to keep going. We must catch him before he crosses the channel." Not only did she want to bring Riku to justice, but now she had to beat him to the top of a mountain.

Gung Lao scrambled for the packs next to him and rummaged around before he felt a few pieces of bread. He handed one to Kwan who took it and tore off a big bite. Then he stood up and dusted himself off with his hand, the other held his own piece of bread, and he chewed as he did so. They rolled up their bedrolls and started again down the path.

Chapter 15

Anyone

"Less than half a day to cross," the boatman said. The middle-aged sailor stood with his back to his wooden seacraft moored at the dock. "Two pieces of silver per passenger." Hiriko looked from Riku to Kasume.

"Seems reasonable," Hiriko said. "When do we depart?"

"We set sail in the morning. The sea gets a bit too rough in the evening even for a ship as fine as *The Blue Shogun*."

Hiriko reached into his pocket for six pieces of silver. Riku stared across the channel as his companions dealt with the crewman. He could not see Hokkaido from his vantage point, as sharp as his eyes were. It was just too far over the horizon. According to the boatman, the waters of the Tsugaru Strait were often rough. The channel separated Honshu from Hokkaido. Riku rarely ever left Honshu and could not remember if he ever had in recent memory. The boatman insisted that to cross the channel, one required a sturdy vessel such as his, though to Riku it looked like nothing more than a small, wooden, single-masted ship, a rickety one at that.

Riku became lost in thought as he looked at the rolling waves over the shore. *They just killed her. Just like that, they killed her. I miss her calm words and her sweet touch. The tangles of her hair. My Yuuki-chan. I'd give anything to have her back. I'd give anything. I wonder if...at the shrine...instead of Unomichi I could...But what of Sakura? I would be one man, twice-married. But my lady Sakura, surely she would understand...wouldn't she? And she's pregnant! Spirits what am I to do?*

Hiriko and Kasume startled him into the present. "We'll have to find some place to spend the night. The boat doesn't leave until morning," said Hiriko.

"I'm hungry, too. Hopefully somewhere with food," Kasume said. Hiriko gave a sigh.

Riku grunted. "It would lift our spirits to get a good meal. Let's find a tavern."

Kasume's face lit up. He all but jumped for joy. "I saw one in town on the main road. I peered in there when we passed it. Maybe they have spare rooms."

Riku crossed his arms and looked over at Hiriko before looking back at Kasume. "Lead the way."

The streets of Omamori town consisted of unpaved packed clay. Dead leaves blew here to there and puddles of muddy water dotted the avenues. The buildings of the town were uneven in their makeup. Some were built of stone while others were built of aged wood worn by the salty sea breeze. Villagers milled about their daily tasks and bowed to one another if they recognized each other, otherwise they ignored them and hurried along their ways. Ninjas were uncommon in this part of the island so the trio gathered a fair share of stares. Often Koga and Iga ninjas alike would try to blend in with the native people but the three of them felt no reason to hide.

They reached the tavern after a short walk. It had a tilted, tiled roof of gray slate. Sliding doors served as walls between its oaken support beams. They could hear laughter and music from inside. "Here we are!" Kasume said, thrilled.

They slid open the door to find several wooden rectangular knee-high tables and *zabuton* seating pads. Several men in robes sat around one of the tables. They laughed and shouted at each other. Many empty small glasses lay on their table; some tipped over and some upright. A few other people, some couples, and a few single men, occupied other tables. Riku and the others picked a vacant table near the back close to the kitchen and waited to be served. Not long after, a hefty man wearing a white apron and a matching white headband came to their table from out of the kitchen.

"Evenin' gentlemen. What are you looking for tonight?"

Riku looked up at him and said, "Two rooms for one night and the best thing on your menu, please."

"Oh, very good. I just happened to have a couple'a rooms open up this morning. And I hope you boys like our seaside ramen. It's the best meal in the whole village."

"Yes please!" Kasume chimed in. "Extra, extra fish and noodles please!"

The waiter chuckled, "You must be hungry, young man."

"And a round of tea for the three of us, please," Hiriko asserted.

"Okay I'll get what you need on the double. And enjoy a glass of sake, on the house for each of you. We don't get travelers like you around here often."

"Thank you, sir," Riku said as he looked up. He looked back down at his companions, but then he noticed one of the men at the crowded table staring at him. When Riku met the man's gaze, the man turned his eyes back to his own party. Like a stone, Riku held his gaze on the man. The man was burly with a strong musculature and an unkempt beard. He had heavy dark circles under his eyes as if he did not sleep well at night. His facial skin was rugged with scars riddling his cheeks. Riku's instincts gave him a bad taste in his mouth, but it was better not to start any trouble.

Their food came and the waiter was truthful, the meal looked delicious. They were each given a huge bowl of ramen with noodles, fish, and four half eggs bathed in broth with many aromatic spices. It was an enormous amount of food. The tea had an autumn leaf aroma to it.

"Gosh, we h'n't had a pro'er meal since we le't the temple!" Kasume said as broth dripped from his mouth.

The three devoured the delicious ramen. Riku caught the bearded man looking at them a handful of times. When they finished their food and drink the waiter showed them to the second floor of the tavern where the rooms were. Riku took one of them for himself while Kasume and Hiriko shared the other. Each room had two beds, a chest and a window that overlooked the alleys and streets below.

Riku made sure his door was locked. He peered out of the window, which afforded him a partially blocked view of the waters of Tsugaru Strait. He crossed his arms and stared at the water.

The demon lord kills innocent people. I must get to him. I must stop him. But how do I even know who he is? He can shapeshift. He could be anybody. How can I trust anyone?!

Yuuki-chan. What did they do to you...what did they do? If only things were different and I could bring you back to life instead. Would Unomichi understand? Would Grandmaster? Would anyone *understand? Or perhaps they'd just call me a fool. Pcht. If I brought her back instead, there would be heavy consequences. It's impossible.*

He rubbed his temple and sighed. He looked out the window to the west and saw the pinks and oranges of the sunset. He shed his robes and collapsed on one of the beds.

/ / /

Iito knelt at the foot of a dark figure. The menacing entity was no more than shadow made flesh. It was wrapped in a robe made of living black moths that covered the being from head to toe. To Iito, the demon lord smelled of carrion left to rot in the sun for weeks.

"Yes, Dark Lord. It would be wise to seize Tiger Claw. As I discovered, it is in the hands of a talented swordswoman named Kwan, a ninja of Iga Temple."

"Go kill her, Ghost of Shō," the dark entity said. "Seize the sword. It would be a powerful weapon in our hands." He shook his robe and three black moths broke away and landed on Iito's shoulder. The moths burrowed into his skin. It was painful but the feeling quickly subsided. "Those moths carry a ward that will protect you from Tiger Claw's suicidal enchantment. Bring the blade to me."

Without looking up, he said, "I will."

Chapter 16

Breath

Many thoughts came and went through Kwan's mind as she and Gung Lao ran down the path. The afternoon sun warmed their faces. She could tell he was exhausted, but they could not stop. He panted and hacked as they went, but he never complained or begged to rest. *I hope we get there in time. Please, Spirits, let us get there in time. I don't want to make Gung Lao follow me to a frigid mountain; not if I can help it. I miss my room back at Iga Temple. I miss Takashi's encouragement and Captain Nobu's harsh lessons. No one is on my side except Gung Lao, and he must follow my orders regardless. I've even earned the ire of Grandmaster Minato of the Koga. Spirits, it's times like these I wish Unomichi was by my side.*

Lost in thought, she neglected to notice how heavy her arms and legs felt and how little breath she had left. The padded robes weren't doing her any favors either. Tiger Claw began to rumble, though she did not quite understand what that meant. The time between rumbles grew shorter and shorter until it would not stop. She slowed to a walk and Gung Lao matched her pace. Now the sword rumbled uncontrollably.

"What's wrong, Mistress?"

"The sword! It's shaking! I don't know what's happening!" She drew it from its sheath, the claw marks began to glow.

Before them on the path a black vertical swipe appeared in midair and split wide. Tiger Claw's gleam heightened into an orange glow like fire. They came to a stop before the portal. A man clad in black robes stepped through with a ninjato strapped to his back.

"*Iito!*" Kwan gasped. "What are you doing here?"

The man snickered and pulled his sword out of its sheath with a hand whose skin was badly burned. "Hand Tiger Claw to me, and I will spare your lives." He reached out towards her with his other burned hand.

"I'll never give it to you. You'll have to kill me to take it from me," she protested. She held the sword in front of her and gripped it firmly while the fiery blade glowed. Gung Lao was visibly terrified but he too pulled out his short sword.

Iito gave a smirk as he held his ninjato before them. Kwan noticed the blade looked oily and discolored. She looked over at Gung Lao who looked back at her. He tightened his jaw as he firmed his grip on his sword.

Iito zipped to Kwan's side and she shifted to face him, Gung Lao at her back. Iito struck at her, his attacks quick and powerful. She was barely quick enough to block them. Gung Lao gritted his teeth and rushed to her side. He lunged his sword at Iito. The ninja batted the attack away. Gung Lao lost his balance and narrowly escaped a return blow as he rolled out of the way. Kwan gave a powerful flurry of overhead and diagonal swings, but Iito blocked or dodged each one of them.

Iito jumped back and tossed pellets at his feet. A black haze burst onto the scene. Gung Lao coughed, "I can't see two feet in front of my face, Mistress!" Kwan could barely see the tip of Tiger Claw herself even though it glowed.

"Stay vigilant, Gung Lao," Kwan said. "Stand with your back to mine. And stay calm. Keep your wits about you." The two waited anxiously as they prepared for their fierce opponent. It was quiet, as if the haze obscured not only vision but dampened sound as well. After a silent moment, Kwan thought she heard the crunch of a footstep. She slashed Tiger Claw in its direction which sent a fire blast toward the sound. The fire disappeared into the haze. They heard a deafening chuckle coming from the opposite direction, to which she replied with another fire blast. The pale sun above was all they had to keep a sense of direction, but even it was almost obscured. "Show yourself, coward," she said into the emptiness. She felt an anxious anger build inside.

"You are unworthy to wield that sword, peasant," Iito's voice intruded.

"Where did that come from? It's like he's coming from all sides! We're in a trap!" Gung Lao bemoaned. His hands shook as he pointed his sword in this direction and that.

"Relax, Gung Lao," Kwan reassured. "We will make it out of here in one piece. Don't lose control." Kwan scanned from left to right, back and forth. Intrusive thoughts came and went from her mind that threatened to steal her attention. *I must remain focused. No more distractions. Iito could appear at any moment.* "You coward! Show yourself!" she said. Her ears steamed.

Gung Lao almost dropped his sword. He wiped the sweat off his face. "I can hear him laughing! He's inside my head! *Gahh!*"

"Weak fools," Iito jibed. He chuckled, again from all directions.

"We can't waste any more time due to your cowardice, Iito," Kwan said. "Now, *show yourself!*" Her anger reached its boiling point. She fed it into her grip on Tiger Claw. The blade's fiery glow grew brighter until the metal itself turned as bright and hot as the sun on a summer day. With one hand she held the sword above her head. A vortex of flame came to life which swirled around them. The flames dissipated the fog. As she peered into the vortex, Kwan swore she could see the shape of an ephemeral tiger that charged within the flames. Gung Lao wondered at the surrounding fiery vortex. The fog was gone. Iito stood on the road, crouched low, ninjato at the ready. The flames had scorched and smoldered the surrounding area.

Kwan held the glowing sword in Iito's direction. She tried to remain calm but she could not contain her heavy breath. She felt the rage burst from her chest. "You want this sword, you menace?! I'll bring it to you!" She held the weapon above her head and charged at him wildly. When she reached her target she brought the sword down with her most powerful strike. The sword hit nothing but ground and its fiery crash exploded as if a meteorite landed before her. Iito leapt up and over her and landed between her and Gung Lao. The servant scrambled to get into a defensive stance as Iito headed for him while Kwan dashed to catch up in desperation.

141

Iito threw a kunai, hitting its mark squarely into Gung Lao's thigh. The man hollered in pain and it broke his concentration. Iito seized the opportunity and cut across Gung Lao's chest. It was a grazing cut, but it would leave a mark. The servant fell to the ground and writhed in pain. Kwan caught up and sent a flurry of swings at Iito with her glowing blade. Iito narrowly dodged each swing and closed the distance. He jabbed Kwan's midsection with his fist. She felt the impact, but there was no time to nurse blows. She hopped back on one foot but with the other heel nailed Iito in the stomach with a strong sidekick. It was such a heavy blow that Iito struggled to get up and started to retch. Kwan took the opportunity to help Gung Lao to his feet. "Come on, big guy. Let's get you out of here." She slung his arm over her shoulder and held Tiger Claw in her free hand. Thinking fast, she reasoned that they wouldn't get far if they simply ran down the path. After she remembered the portal Iito left behind, she touched the opening with the glowing sword. *To the north. Bring us to the north* she whispered in her head. Tiger Claw gave a strong jolt of feedback before its vibrations stopped completely. They stepped through the portal.

/ / /

Kwan felt the temperature shift before she noticed anything else. It was so cold here she could see the puffs of her breath. When she came out of the portal she fell face first into a puddle of mud in an alleyway between old cabins made of gray lumber from trees long dead. Gung Lao lay next to her unconscious and his breath was shallow. She bent over him and lightly tapped his face to see if he would wake up. Gung Lao bled from his chest and needed healing fast. "Gung Lao! Gung Lao wake up! Wake up dang you!" She jiggled his head a little and his eyes opened a sliver.

"Mistress...where are we?" he said weakly. He gave two belabored coughs.

"Don't speak Gung Lao. I'll find help. Try to keep yourself awake." She dragged his body out of the mud against one of the cabins in the alley. She painted a mental picture of his location and ran between the cabins onto a main street. It was still the afternoon and many people milled about. They wore different colored padded robes, kimonos, and street attire for the chilly weather. Some of them looked at her with disgust as her cherry-blossom print black robes were covered head to toe in mud. She came up to the closest person. It was a middle-aged man.

"Good sir. Is there a healer somewhere in town?" she asked, half in a panic. The man grumbled and ignored her and went about his business. She tried more citizens, this time a young couple. "Please, can you help me? My friend is gravely injured, I need to take him to a healer. Where is it?" The young man looked to his partner and back at Kwan.

"The healer is just down the main road," he said. "Look for the vial and stitches sign. Can't miss it." He pointed down the road and she could just make out a wooden sign of that description.

"Thank you, thank you a thousand times. Thank you." She weaved her way through the crowd as quickly as she could toward the sign. The healer's building was an old cabin that did not stand out much from the surrounding ones. It had a pair of swing doors for easy access and she passed through them. Before she looked around she cried, "Help! Someone! My attendant is badly injured! Help!" She panicked and her heart beat out of her chest.

A medical attendant looked up from one of the many bedsides and he came over to her briskly. He was a tall, lanky-looking man with shortly trimmed dark hair. "What's going on? Is someone injured?" he asked.

"Yes! Thank you! My traveling partner. He's injured. He's in an alleyway not far away."

"I see," the man said. He looked over his shoulder and called, "Gyoji-san! Grab three others and bring the litter." He looked back at Kwan. "Lead the way to him, miss."

As the attendant Gyoji gathered more attendants, Kwan asked the man, "Sir, what town is this? Where are we?"

He gave her a quizzical look. "You mean you don't know? This is Omamori."

"Forgive me, where is that?"

"Geographically, we're at the northernmost end of the main island of Honshu. Are you alright, miss? I mean spiritually."

"Yeah, I'm fine. We were…attacked on the road by bandits. We narrowly escaped."

"I see. Ah. Bandits…in Omamori…right…Are you sure you're okay miss? You didn't bump your head, did you? Ah, the orderlies are ready. My name is Ruka, by the way. Lead the men to the patient." The stout man named Gyoji and three others came to her with a medical litter. She led them outside and back between the cabins into the alley. There Gung Lao lay. He took shallow breaths. The men moved him onto the litter and with two on each end they carried him back to the healer's cabin and Kwan ran alongside.

When they reached the healer's cabin, they placed Gung Lao on a feather bed. Gung Lao sighed but the saliva that dripped from the side of his mouth was black. The healers examined him. They collected a sample of it and put it into a vial that contained a transparent solution. As the healer swirled it around, the solution darkened, but in a few seconds it turned amber. Then, the healer consulted with Ruka. After they talked it over for a moment, Ruka came to Kwan who was seated on a zabuton cushion in the corner.

"It looks like he was poisoned," Ruka said. "But the wound is fresh. Our healers can likely save his life."

Kwan gave a sigh of relief. Ruka continued, "Though, it will likely take several weeks for him to recover. There are a few taverns in town. I am sure they have spare rooms available for you if you wish to wait."

"Kwan-san," Gung Lao uttered from the bed, his voice weak. She approached his bed. "Mistress what's my condition?"

"Gung Lao! You're in bad shape, my friend," she said. "But they said you will make a full recovery. I'll have to wait for you here while you recover."

"But…that would mean Riku walks free. And our mission will fail." He gave labored coughs.

"I guess…yes. That's what that means."

"No, I will not allow it," he said. More coughs. "You will not fail on my account. You must finish it. Promise me you'll complete our mission."

"I'm pleased you're calling it *our* mission, Gung Lao." She saw him crack a smile.

"You must bring Riku to justice. You must avenge Unomichi-san. It is your duty." Gung Lao passed out.

Kwan mulled over what Gung Lao said. She wanted to stay with him, but he was right. She could not let Riku go unpunished. Unomichi had to be avenged. "Ruka-san, when does the next ship depart for Hokkaido?"

"Well, at the harbor, there is one boat that makes the crossing early every morning. *The Blue Shogun*. But it would have already left for the day." Kwan sighed. They were too late. Riku probably already made the crossing. She would have to cross as well. And worse, she would have to do it alone. She had no choice but to wait until tomorrow morning. *Maybe someone's seen him. It's not often a Koga ninja wanders this far north. And perhaps he wasn't even lying low. It couldn't hurt to ask around if anyone had seen him.*

"Which way is the harbor?" she asked him.

"If you follow the main road further down as far as it goes, it ends at the harbor. Now, we need to focus on healing your partner, so excuse me."

"Of course," she replied. She gave the unconscious Gung Lao one last look before she left the medical cabin.

Back out on the streets, her panic calmed, Kwan more readily noticed the cold settle into her skin especially around her neck and face. The dried mud still clung to her clothes. She felt at her side for Tiger Claw. The sword's warmth stilled her shivers. She looked left and right at the passing crowds of villagers. Several men carried nets over their shoulders filled with their daily catches. With some time to kill she thought she would inspect the harbor and make sure she knew where it was for the next morning. She entered the crowd and turned north. Tiger Claw at her waist sat calmly in its sheath. Its rumbles subsided. After she followed the flow of the crowd between rows of log cabin buildings built from the same aged lumber mixed with other stone buildings, she finally made it to the harbor. She stared across Tsugaru Strait under the overcast sky toward Hokkaido.

Kwan gasped. In the distance atop the water she made out a brown object that tossed gently side to side. *That must be the transport vessel.*

"Riku!" she called to the vessel. *"I will bring you to justice! I will!"*

Chapter 17

Cornered

"Zeshiro, what is the meaning of this?" Grandmaster Minato asked the demon. They stood in the courtyard of Koga Temple near the still waters of the pond under the cherry blossom tree, its flowers beautifully bloomed in pink blossoms. Beside the Grandmaster of the temple stood Goro and Daisuke as well as two more ninjas, all of them dressed in their casual white robes.

"She was killed by a servant of the demon lord." Zeshiro said. "This I swear."

"I can confirm this, Grandmaster," Aurabos said. "We followed the sorceress, Chi, and found her dragging Yuuki's corpse through Onigawa."

Daisuke scratched his chin. "To think that Chi was a traitor, a servant of the demon lord. And right under our noses."

"She seemed mischievous since the moment I met her," the bulky ninja Goro said. "She always had calculating eyes that studied everything around her."

"What were the circumstances under which you had met her, Grandmaster?" Zeshiro asked.

Minato said, "She appeared one day, perhaps ten years ago, asking for refuge. We didn't ask any questions and obliged. We had no reason to suspect her of being an enemy. She was just…a regular woman. She soon after fell in love with Unomichi."

"She was a spy from the beginning. The demon lord stole her as a small child and brought her up as his pupil. He taught her dark magic, then planted her here when she was ready," Zeshiro said. "Quite a malicious story, if you ask me."

"How unfortunate for her and for us," Minato said. "She must have been his source of information for the decade or so she lived with us. She had a son with Unomichi. Yenfay is his name."

"What will become of him? Both of his parents are gone," Zeshiro asked. "Surely his mother poisoned his mind against the Koga."

"We have no reason to believe that," Minato reassured. "He is still quite young, just ten years old. We have begun training him as a Koga ninja. He seems quite prodigious."

"It is my recommendation you kill him. Just to be sure," Zeshiro said.

Minato's eyes widened and the Koga ninjas fell silent as they searched for each other's reactions. "Out of the question. He remains one of us. Absolutely not."

"If you insist," Zeshiro said. "But there may come a day he will betray you. It is a risk."

"We will happily take that chance on the boy," Daisuke said. Zeshiro turned his head and looked at the ninja that chimed in.

"You humans take too many chances," Zeshiro said coldly.

"Indeed," Daisuke responded equally coldly, staring Zeshiro directly in the eyes.

Minato shattered the uncomfortable silence. "Enough. Goro-san, gather servants and take Yuuki-san's body to the graveyard and have her buried."

"Yes Grandmaster," Goro answered.

"Now, where will you go next, demon?" Minato asked.

"We will continue our hunt for the demon lord. He means to rule the human realm and must be stopped. He knows we're after him and he can change forms, so he is incredibly hard to track down. We had a close call, but he saw us coming."

"Mm," Minato mulled. "Remember what Grandmaster Tei said: follow the insects."

/ / /

Kwan wandered into the tavern closest to the harbor. It looked older than most of the other buildings in town, perhaps because it was so close to the sea and the salty breezes wore away at the already grayed timber walls. A swinging wooden sign read *The Uchi Mata Inn*. It was held up by rusted iron hooks. She was glad to get out of the cold. When she walked through the door, a stiff wintery breeze from behind blew her hair into her face. The room was dark since her eyes had not yet adjusted to the warm lighting of the tavern's interior, but she could make out several tables filled with fishermen enjoying their time on shore over a warm cup of tea. At the far end of the main floor was a bar counter that the barkeeper busied herself behind. She was a stout woman with the musculature like that of a fit man. She wore a plain white shirt and a brown vest with sewn-on pockets with black buttons. She struck Kwan as someone who would fare well in a brawl.

Kwan walked gingerly to the counter and tried to keep the men in the corners of her eyes in case they tried anything. A few of the men gave passing glances at her, but none said anything. After Kwan made it to the counter, the barkeeper said, "G'day miss. What d'ya need? Care for a drink? Or per'aps a room? Our rooms 'ave locks on the doors, so there'll be no funny business."

"Yes I'll be needing a room. Just for one night." Kwan looked over her shoulder. Some of the men had started to watch her. She looked back at the barkeeper. "A room with the sturdiest lock, please. And a decent washroom. As you can tell, I'm a little muddy."

"A'course. And what be bringin' ya to town, miss?" She looked down at the glass she rubbed with a white rag that had seen better days.

"I'm, uh, looking for someone."

"Hm. Someone in particular? Or d'ya mean a lover?"

Kwan gave a snort. "Both, I guess you could say."

The barkeeper put down the glass, picked up another one, and began to rub it. "Men're a blade a' grass in a field, especially for a pretty one like yourself miss."

"Not this one," Kwan said more to herself than the barkeeper. "He's special to me. He's strong, noble, and brave. He makes me feel special. Worthy. Beautiful." She looked over her shoulder and out of the window at the waves in the distance. "And he was taken from me."

151

The barkeeper didn't know what to say so she continued to rub glasses with her rag and looked out the window with her. Kwan turned back to the barkeeper and said, "Did you see a man dressed like a *shinobi* come through here?"

"A *shinobi*? A ninja, ya mean." At that, even more of the men looked up at her, some with their backs turned looked over their shoulders. "Hm. Can't say that I 'ave," she said. "Hey Komoda!" she yelled to one of the patrons. "You seen a ninja come through here?"

A particularly unsettling man looked up from his table. "Who's asking?" Komoda was tall, burly, and strong. Scars riddled his cheeks beneath his unkempt beard. He looked as if he never stopped eating and he reeked of alcohol.

"This lass here," the barkeeper said. "Erm, what was your name, miss?"

Pausing a moment Kwan turned and talked to the barkeeper with her eyes on the patron Komoda, "My name is not important. Now, did you come across a ninja? Named Riku?"

The patron at the table scowled. "I said 'Who's asking?' What don't you understand? And aye, you're a pretty young thing. What if I took you to 'im?"

"That won't be necessary. Just tell me what you know and I'll be on my way." She felt a sinking feeling deep in her core from her heart to her stomach. She covered Tiger Claw's handle. Two men came from either side and grabbed both of her arms. They were too large to shake free of.

"Let her go! And get out of here, the lot of you! Go on, get out of here! I'm getting the town guards!" the barkeeper cried.

She dropped the rag and made her way out of the front door in search of help.

Komoda grunted. "Let's take her out back. Aye you are a pretty one." Kwan struggled but it was no use. The harder she thrashed the firmer the men held. Seven of them in all escorted her through the rear exit toward the alley.

"Unhand me, bastards! Unhand me!" she yelled. They took her outside into the muddy alleyway. She finally shook her right arm free. Acting quickly, she empty-hand struck the throat of the man that gripped her other arm. Fenced in by the buildings, she'd have to fight her way out. She backed away from them and drew Tiger Claw. The men each took out their hooked fishing knives.

"Now look here, missy," Komoda said. "There's seven of us men against your tiny self, so throw down your weapon."

She counteracted, "You'll tell me where Riku is and you'll regret attacking me, if you live past the next minute, that is."

"We're not telling you a dang thing, miss. And *we're* the ones making the demands, not you."

"You come any closer and I'll chop off pieces of you you'll surely miss." She felt her blood begin to boil. From the bottom of her eye, she noticed the marks on Tiger Claw begin to glow. She held the sword at eye level. The glowing marks were so bright, they hurt. One of the burly fishermen stepped toward her and reeled back his dagger. Kwan stepped forward and plunged her sword through his belly. He fell to his knees and she pulled out the blade. The man fell facedown into the mud, lifeless. The other six men shared nervous glances. Another charged her and

153

before he could bring down his dagger, Kwan sidestepped and cut off the dagger hand. In one fluid motion she spun around and beheaded him. She flicked the blood off the sword and hopped back to put some distance between herself and the attackers. Two more of them came after her. The first gave a lunging stab at her face but she ducked the blow and struck him with a sidekick that knocked him to the muddy ground. The other attacker grabbed her shoulder and went for a stab but she caught his wrist and thrust Tiger Claw through his forearm. He dropped the knife and fell to his knees. She pulled out the sword and stabbed him through the heart.

The other attacker scrambled in the mud for his knife, but before he could pick it up, Kwan leapt and pierced him through his back until Tiger Claw met the ground. The man gave a last gasp.

Komoda ordered, "Go on, the two of you! Attack her!" The last two men threw down their daggers and fled. "Where are you going?!" he called after them. When he turned back to face Kwan he found her holding her sword to his throat. He soiled himself and fell to his knees.

"Please don't kill me, miss! I'll tell you anything you want to know! Just…please! Please don't kill me!" Komoda dropped his weapon as Kwan held the sword to his neck.

"This is the legendary blade Tiger Claw. If you'd just told me where you'd seen him, you wouldn't be in this mess. Now, have you seen the ninja Riku?" Her voice became a fierce growl, "*Tell me what I want to know!*"

"I saw him! I saw him. He left this morning on *The Blue Shogun* to cross the channel. He was with two other young ninjas. That's all I know! Now please...please don't kill me," he pleaded.

"Thank you," Kwan replied, "but you tried to ruin me, and I can't let you carry on." She took a step back and sent a burst of flame at the kneeling man. She placed Tiger Claw back in its sheath and stood for a moment to watch the man burn to death.

Chapter 18

Passage

Hiriko spent most of his time aboard *The Blue Shogun* puking over the side of the wooden vessel. At first, Kasume cracked jokes, pointed, and laughed at him. But as the trip wore on he grew worried and tried to offer his friend some consolation. "We're almost to shore. Nearly there," he told him. In the distance, Hokkenzen Mountain loomed atop the island with its mountainsides covered in snow. Riku watched the mountain grow as they approached.

I must find some plan of action to reach the shrine near the summit. Perhaps there is already a pathway.

Besides Riku's group there was a merchant aboard the vessel as well as an elderly couple. He decided he would try to gather as much information as he could from them about Hokkaido. He would start with the merchant.

He was a round man that wore a green shirt and golden robes. He had several sturdy trunks that contained wares he intended to sell on the far side of the channel. He sat atop one as he looked over the sides of the vessel.

"How fares you sir?" Riku asked the merchant.

The man looked over his shoulder at Riku who was dressed in his black robes, sword strapped to his back. "Aye, I've been better. At least, better than your friend over there," he indicated to Hiriko who braced the side of the vessel. "Is he gonna be okay?"

"First time at sea for the young man. He'll be fine."

"I hope so," the merchant chuckled. "I remember my first time at sea. It was with my father as we made this very same trip across the channel."

"Do you make this trip often?"

"Hai, countless times. My fares have all but paid for this vessel twice over."

"Oh? And what are you selling?"

"I sell toys, jewelry, and trinkets at the market at the far side of the channel."

"It's my first time travelling to Hokkaido. Can you tell me about the area?"

"Well, sure. It gets quite cold all over the island this time of year. You'd be wise to purchase some warmer clothing. The harbor town is called Hakazu. The biggest city on the island, Opporo it's called, is a nice town with a big marketplace, though it's further north on the west side of the island. It's close to the path to the mountain. I sell there on special occasions. The snow festival and the sun festival and the like."

"Ahh the mountain path you say?" Riku quipped. "My companions and I are sightseers and wish to get up close to the mountains."

"Ah, a company of fine taste. Opporo is your destination then! Yes the path from there leads to Hokkenzen Mountain. Now that you mention it, if you stop in at the famous hot springs a little ways up the path, tell them Gishi sent you. They'll treat you right, guaranteed."

"This has been a most profitable conversation, Gishi. Thank you."

Gishi cleared his throat and held out his palm. Riku took his hand and shook it. Gishi's hand went limp. "No sir I meant; can I have a few coins? I am a merchant after all and information isn't free. I must pay fees. You understand, don't you?"

Riku sighed heavily, "Alright fine." He took out his pouch and pulled out two silver coins and placed them into Gishi's palm.

"Pleasure doing business," Gishi said as he opened his own pouch and dropped the coins in with a dull *clink*. He turned his head back over his shoulder to watch the waves. The pair of deckhands of *The Blue Shogun* busied themselves. They fastened ropes and hurried to and fro on the craft. The captain stood at the wheel, keeping the boat on course. The water was not particularly choppy but it fought him enough to keep him at the wheel.

The elderly couple sat facing each other on wooden crates at the side of the craft. They had a somber look to them. The old woman wore gray robes with a white shift underneath. She leaned on her husband with her head under his chin as she held back tears. The old man similarly wore gray robes, a shade darker than his wife's. As *The Blue Shogun* rose and fell against the waves, Riku watched them from afar. He could not help but become lost in thoughts of himself and Yuuki. The melancholic looks on their faces struck his heartstrings. *That could have been me and Yuuki feeling sad over something there. But I'll never have that with her. There was something about Yuuki, something about her way. The way she used to be so effortlessly pleasant. Stubborn yet fair. She always had a warm smile when I looked into her eyes. The way they just...killed her like that. Unforgiveable. What would it matter to anyone if I brought her back instead of Unomichi?*

As if they could read his mind, the old man tenderly rubbed his wife's shoulder and looked over at Riku. Realizing he was staring, Riku shook himself awake and darted his eyes over the side.

I suppose if I still had Yuuki, I wouldn't have Sakura. She's truly a blessing. Really she's all that's gotten me through this... Yet still, she was my Yuuki—"

"Young man," Riku heard from over his shoulder. Riku turned and saw that the old man beckoned him. "Young man come here please. Come here." Riku gingerly approached.

"Yes hello sir."

"Young man I overheard you are going to make the journey up Hokkenzen Mountain," the old man said. "Is this true?" The old woman looked up at her husband then at Riku with a new light in her eyes.

"Well, yes. My companions and I are looking to do some sightseeing. We heard the view from the mountains there is most beautiful."

The old man stood up and reached into an inside pocket in his robes. He took out something wrapped in hide cloth. "Young man, my wife is very sick. Very, very sick. None of the many

159

healers we have been to have been able to cure her in the slightest. Our only hope is to make an offering to the spirits. It is said that the more difficult it is to travel to a shrine, the more potent the offering."

"I see," Riku said.

"There is a shrine atop Hokkenzen Mountain. It is said to be one of the most difficult to reach in all of Japan. As you can see, we are very old and frail and cannot make the journey." He unwrapped the object and revealed what looked like a bundle of tiny bones. Looking closer, Riku could see that the bones were tied together in the shape of a scroll. "Scored onto these bones is a sacred inscription."

"Hmm. You want us to bring this...scroll to Hokkenzen Shrine?"

"Yes, young man. Yes. Though, I have next to nothing to offer you. Merely the blessings of an old couple."

Riku paused for a moment to think it over. *We're going there anyway. We might as well help these old people out. I suppose it couldn't hurt.*

"As it turns out, my companions and I were planning to visit the shrine anyway. It would be no trouble at all to lend you a hand," Riku said.

The old man looked over to his wife and cheered, "Do you hear that Ama? The young man and his friends will visit the shrine for us." She began to smile. He turned back to Riku and softly placed the bone scroll in its wrappings into Riku's palms with a bright smile. "May the spirits bless you with all good things, young man. Err, what was your name?"

160

"Riku. My name is Riku."

"Riku-san, this is no ordinary scroll. No, it contains a magical spell. Since you are so kind, visiting the shrine in our stead will be enough for us. Instead, you may use the scroll."

Riku blinked. "But what does it do?"

"When the time comes, you will know. Thank you." The old man bowed, then turned, sat back down, and smiled with his wife. Riku looked at the object in his hands nestled in the hide cloth. The bones had scores in them but the symbols were illegible. He could sense a faint hint of soothing energy seep from them into his hands. He wrapped the bundle of bones and placed it into his pouch.

Over his shoulder, Riku heard Hiriko retch again. Kasume was rubbing his back worried. He went to them. "I've discovered a way up the mountain. We need to reach Opporo. It's on the western side of the island. The merchant said there's a path that leads up to Hokkenzen Mountain. It's our best option."

Hiriko looked up at Riku, clearly exhausted and dehydrated. "Okay. If it's our best option, let's go there."

"You'll be fine once we reach the harbor, Hiriko," Riku consoled. "We're nearly there." They looked over the bow of the ship and could make out the harbor of Hakazu in the distance. Hokkenzen Mountain loomed behind.

/ / /

Daisuke was surprised at how adept Akari and Mizu were at learning hand-to-hand combat skills. It seemed to him that whenever he stumbled upon them they were practicing moves on each other. But they did not practice how one might expect kids would. They did not chase each other around or giggle. It seemed to him they honed each move to become as efficient as possible. Out of the young ninjutsu students, Akari and Mizu were number one and number two at their rank, with Yenfay a close third.

In her first training mission, Akari was to sneak into Grandmaster Minato's office unnoticed and pilfer just one of his prized porcelain teacups. If successful, Minato would allow her to keep it. No student had ever successfully completed this mission before. How could they? They were novices and the Grandmaster was very careful. Akari would have been successful had she followed directions and taken only one cup. In the moment, she wanted to take an additional cup so Mizu could have one too. Minato discovered the misstep and deemed the attempt a failure due to not following the mission objective, though he could not help but feel impressed by her resourcefulness and he let her keep the teacups anyway on the condition that she learn the tea ceremony. She quite liked tea so she decided to accept his offer. He reminded her that before she knew it, she would perform in her first belt test. Even though she hated tests, her heart was beating calmly and the thought of ranking up was more of a relief than anything else.

Mizu's arrow hit the tree target. It was the last of her arrows. "Akari-chan, can you fetch the arrows again?" Mizu asked.

"Yes Mizu-chan. I'm on it," Akari replied. She ran across the forest clearing. The afternoon sun shined bright. She began gathering the few arrows that had gone astray. Then she went to the tree Mizu targeted and pulled them out. "That's seven hits and five misses!" she called to Mizu on the far side of the clearing. "You've gotten much better!"

From behind Mizu, they heard Yenfay say, "I can do better than that, Akari-chan."

As she pulled out the arrows she smiled to herself. "You think you can do better than Mizu-chan?" Akari said as she ran to them, quiver full of arrows. "Put your money where your mouth is. You have to beat seven hits. Think you can do it?" She shoved the quiver against the boy's chest.

"No question. And if I win, you have to kiss me on the cheek, Akari-chan."

"Kiss you on the cheek?! Ugh fine, I guess," she blushed. She looked over at Mizu who gasped in disbelief. "But if you don't hit more than seven, you have to make our beds for a week!"

"Deal. No sweat," Yenfay said. Mizu handed him the bow. He looked downrange and took a deep breath. He knocked the first arrow, aimed, and let it loose. It fell short of the tree by a few feet. The girls giggled.

"That was just a practice shot." He knocked his second arrow, pulled back, and shot it right on target. He did the same with the next arrow and the next. Every arrow hit the target. Dumbfounded, Akari and Mizu looked at each other. Secretly Akari hoped he could do it. She admired his confident attitude.

"I can't believe he beat me," Mizu said, "but a deal's a deal." She pushed Akari toward Yenfay. Blush covered Akari's face.

Her jaw trembled as she approached. Yenfay held the bow at his side and waited for her.

C'mon Akari. You can kiss him, she thought, trying to convince herself. *You can throw him around and punch him and kick him in training. How hard is it to just kiss him? Oh, I'm so nervous. What if I screw it up? Will he hate me? Ugh, better to just get on with it.*

As Akari approached, Yenfay closed his eyes. She leaned in and pecked him on the cheek. He giggled and looked at her. She smiled and avoided his gaze. He blushed almost as much as Akari. He dropped the bow and quiver and gave her a hug. He looked her in the eye before he ran away through the trees toward the temple.

Akari looked to Mizu who said, "Oh spirits! You kissed him!"

"I had to Mizu-chan! We lost the bet!"

"You liked it too!"

Akari hit her friend on the arm. "I did not!" she said. "He's just a stupid boy."

"Yeah. *Okay* Akari-chan. Hey, when's the wedding?" They laughed together and gossiped to each other about Yenfay and Akari the rest of the afternoon beneath the pine trees.

Chapter 19

Hakazu

She awoke to the sound of birds chirping outside the window. It was the first time in several nights Kwan slept on a proper bed. After she rubbed the sleepiness out of her eyes she gasped in a panic. The sun outside her window was high in the sky. It was already midday.

"The Blue Shogun!" she cried to herself. She leapt out of the bed. "Spirits! I've overslept!" She threw her robes over her slip and shoved her feet into her slippers. She tore open her bedroom door and hurried down the stairs as she clambered to strap Tiger Claw to her waist.

As she blew past the bar counter, the barkeeper said, "What's the rush honey?"

"No time!" Kwan yelled over her shoulder as she made a dash out of *The Uchi Mata Inn.* It was a pleasant enough day but Kwan could pay the nice climate little attention. The boulevard was busy with foot traffic and horse-drawn carts. She hassled through it. She bobbed and weaved between people and fended off bothered glances. She felt as if she were being tossed about. She finally reached the harbor at the end of the road, but *The Blue Shogun* wasn't there. Dock hands carried boxes of goods here and there. She asked one of them where the craft was.

"Aye *The Shog'n*? It left hours ago, miss. It be leavin' again tomorrow mornin' as it does e'ry day. Try again t'morrow, miss."

"*Seven curses!*" Kwan screamed. *If only I'd been more careful about waking up on time. That blasted Riku keeps getting further ahead. I'll never catch him at this rate.*

She cleared her throat and tried to regain poise in front of the deckhand despite her lack of it just then. She turned away and sighed. *I suppose I'll pay a visit to Gung Lao in the meantime. But first, back to the inn.*

She trudged back through the crowded roadway to *The Uchi Mata Inn* with a grim, indignant face. When she reached it, she sat down at the bar counter. Behind it, the barkeeper arranged glasses.

"A glass of shochu please," Kwan ordered.

"Coming right up," the barkeeper said.

"Can I take the glass to my room?"

Sensing how upset she was, she replied, "Yeah of course," and poured her a glass. Kwan immediately gulped down the small glass of alcohol. Its nutty flavor reminded her of the alcohol sold in Prima Village.

"Another, please," Kwan ordered. The barkeeper gingerly poured her another glass. Kwan grabbed it and took it away from the table. She trudged up the stairs to her room. When she reached it, she closed the door behind her and sat down on the bed. She didn't often drink midday but she figured she might as well. She took a swig of the liquor. It tasted strong. Good. She set the drink down and collapsed back onto the bed. *Gung Lao isn't going anywhere. I'll just have a nap.* As she stared at the ceiling, she began to hum a song she learned a long time ago. Tears filled her eyes as she hummed and sniffled. The song reminded her of home. Soon she sang the words.

Outside the village begins the forest
Out there my lover has gone so far
Oh where, oh where has my lover off gone
My lover has gone, has gone to war

I feel his voice on cool spring breeze
It fills my heart with sorrow
I know it's his breath that speaks to me
Bring him back to me tomorrow

When will the sun rise again
When will the darkness go
I pray someday the war will end
And love again I'll know

I know not if he'll come back to me
Or if he's already passed
I hope and beg and pray each day
He will return at last

Kwan's tears wouldn't stop as she struggled through the song.

One day, one day my love will return
And fill our home with love
For now I look in the distance and wait
For one day, that day will come

She gave a whimper and sat up on the side of the bed. She reached over to the bedside table and grabbed her glass of shochu. She took a sizeable gulp before she crashed back down.

/ / /

Riku and Kasume delicately brought Hiriko off the wooden ramp of *The Blue Shogun* onto the docks of Hakazu, each with an arm over his shoulders. He looked gray since he had lost a lot of fluids, but as soon as his foot touched the solid dock a new vitality rushed through him.

"Kasume-kun, go find him some fresh water and somewhere to get a bite to eat," Riku ordered. "I'm going to sit at the dock here with Hiriko-kun awaiting your return. He seems weak."

"I'm not weak! I'm just a little shaky is all!" Hiriko protested.

"You need energy. You can't go on in this condition. Now sit." Riku pointed to a bench at the base of the dock. He and Hiriko slowly made their way over to it while Kasume ran ahead into the town of Hakazu. The harbor only consisted of six wooden docks that extended various lengths. *The Blue Shogun* was moored at the dock furthest to the east which gave Kasume the longest way to travel into the town. At the base of the dock was a heavy thicket of bushes that separated the harbor deck from the town. Scruffy-looking sailors were busy at work. They tied ropes and carried heavy boxes off transport ships and onto wooden carts. As Kasume made his way past a group of them, they eyed him coldly and gave him a sense of unease. He brushed them off and made his way off the wooden deck into Hakazu. The town was little more than a fishing village. The few villagers he came across did not pay him any heed. Kasume presumed they regularly came across travelers whom they would never see again so, like an unnoticed breeze, the town denizens paid them no attention. The villagers wore clothing suited for cold temperatures. Thick woolen coats over multiple layers. Kasume realized it was colder in Hakazu. He warily walked at a brisque pace through the avenues as he looked for an inn or bar, anywhere they served water.

Finally, he came across an inn. The building was made of aged wood, not unlike that in Omamori back across the channel. It would have had an appealing Japanese style exterior if not for its aged paneling. He made his way inside.

The *shoji* sliding doors were heavier than they appeared. And Kasume all but made a fool of himself when he tried to slide them open and close them behind himself. The room was dimly lit by candles. There were several tables of people there listening to a *geisha* play a samisen. A servant briskly made her way from table to table to collect teacups and plates of food.

"Excuse me miss, I need to purchase jars of water, if you have them. And maybe some beef and some cheese."

"Mmm, we have no beef here, only fish," the waitress said. "And we certainly have water we can sell you." The samisen continued to play.

Behind Kasume the shoji door slid open and Hiriko and Riku appeared at the door. "We followed you here," Hiriko said.

"He got restless and went after you," Riku said.

Kasume felt a little annoyed. "I wish you'd just trusted me to get it done."

"Well, we're here now. Sorry," Riku said. "Let's get a table." The three of them found an unoccupied wooden table and each sat on a *zabuton* cushion. Riku signaled to the waitress and ordered three glasses of hot tea and a pitcher of water. The three of them silently listened to the geisha's songs. The delicate plucking of strings brought a pleasant stillness to their tired hearts. Riku remembered the last time he listened to a samisen. It was shortly before the last time he saw Yuuki. The music brought him mixed nostalgic emotions of sadness and happiness with the shifting of memories.

The three of them ate all the sushi they could. It must have been the fanciest establishment in the village because the fish was fresh caught and full of flavor without a hint of salt.

"I recognize you," a man's voice said to them from the table behind. "You're Riku-san of the Koga." The three of them looked over their shoulders at the voice's source. It was a hooded man that wore brown travelers clothing. He sat by himself with his back against the wall. With a gloved hand the man took a sip of his tea.

"I'm not Riku. Who are you?" Riku said as his hand covered the sword handle at his hip.

"Peace, Riku-san," the man said. "I am a friend. I come from Opporo." Riku stole a glance at Hiriko and another at Kasume.

Kasume whispered to Hiriko, "Did he say 'Opporo'?"

"Yes I'm from Opporo. I came looking for assistance."

"What kind of assistance?" Riku said brusquely. "Speak."

The hooded fellow looked around the room then said, "This is not a safe place to discuss it."

"That's too bad," Riku protested. "We're not following you anywhere. Discuss it here, or begone."

The man drew a sigh and fell silent. Then he said, "Very well. The Daimyo of Opporo sent me to find help. My name is Shin. He told me that he would release me from jail if I found help. So here I am."

Riku's brow furled. "What were you in jail for?"

"Burglary," Shin said. "I'm a thief by trade." The sounds of the samisen plucked at a gentle pace that filled the room with a relaxed feeling. She plucked the strings with meticulous skill and drew much attention. The people at the tables listened to the music in silence or chatted with each other and kept to their own conversations. It was a pleasant atmosphere.

"What is it you need help with?" Hiriko asked.

"Ronin thugs took control of the city. They've been brutalizing the citizens. Their gang boss installed posts at every entrance of Opporo. No one is allowed in or out unless they pay a heavy fine."

"What if they don't pay the fine?" Kasume asked.

"You'll see," Shin said. He took a deep sip from his teacup. The geisha plucked away at her samisen at a more rapid pace. It was a frantic piece that filled one with a feeling of discomfort before it resolved again into a relaxed melody. "You are ninjas of the Koga. You can help in ways that no one else can. We need you to destroy them by…removing…their leader."

"I see," Riku said.

"We have the schematics of the building the ronin boss resides in," Shin continued. "We have reached the end of what I am at liberty to tell you in a public place like this."

Riku asked, "And why should we help you? What business is it of ours?"

"I understand you are heading to Hokkenzen Mountain? The ronin have fortified the mountain path. They're letting no one through, regardless of whether the traveler pays the toll. Even Koga ninjas such as yourselves couldn't get through. Now I've said too much."

"How did you know—?" Kasume said.

"Don't think too hard about it. You stick out like a sore thumb here," Shin said. Kasume gave Hiriko an offended look. Shin continued, "So, I know a hidden passageway in and out of Opporo we can use under cover of darkness. Will you accept?"

The three Koga ninjas looked at each other. Riku said, "We'll need to talk this over."

"My room is up the stairs and at the end of the hall, last door on the left. Meet me there in twenty minutes. Make sure no one follows you." He downed the last of his tea and wiped his mouth on his sleeve before he left the main room. He made his way up the stairs out of sight.

At a whisper, Hiriko said, "I don't like this."

Kasume responded, "I think we should at least hear him out. It sounds like these ronin stand in our way."

"It is risky," Riku said, "but our objectives do intersect. I doubt the three of us alone could fight our way through heavy fortifications. This could be our only way forward."

Kasume sniffed. "We should do it. We are Koga ninjas. We help those in need."

Hiriko crossed his arms and said, "If you want to hear him out, then fine. I still think it's a needless risk."

"We'll speak with him and then decide," Riku said. After a few minutes, the waitress came back to collect their plates.

"Do you have any vacancies? We need two rooms," Riku said.

"Of course, sir. We have several available," she said. Riku left the cost of their meals on the table and the three of them followed her up the stairs. She handed them two keys and introduced them to their rooms, Kasume and Hiriko together and Riku on his own. They placed their belongings down in their respective rooms. Hiriko and Kasume went to Riku's room and after they waited a few minutes more they made their way to the end of the hallway to Shin's room. Once there, they knocked. Shin opened the door a crack and, once he confirmed it was them, hurried them into the room. He had a large, unfurled map on his bed. Riku looked closer but did not recognize the area.

"This is a map of Opporo," Shin said. "Do you see here?" he pointed to a spot on the map near the bottom. "This here is the southern entrance. It's the closest entrance to us now." He shook his head. "Off limits. Too many ronin guards. Off to the northeast," he touched a spot in the top right, "is the beginning of the path to Hokkenzen Mountain. It's fortified. Many ronin guards patrol day and night. But look here." He pointed to a spot to the southeast outside the city walls. "Hidden in the trees is the mouth of an old escape route. I used it to leave Opporo."

"Where does the other end let out specifically?" Riku asked, arms crossed.

"It lets out behind the stables of the castle under a trapdoor. It's within the castle walls."

"Castle? The ronin boss resides in a castle?" Kasume exclaimed.

"Yes. Boss Kojiro kicked the Daimyo out of the castle. But once we deal with him, his men will surely scatter. Fortunately, I have personally burgled Opporo Castle many times, so I know the ins and outs. But I'm no fighter. If I tried to assassinate Boss Kojiro, I'd surely be captured."

"So, that's why you need our help," Hiriko said. "Riku-san, I don't think it's wise to get involved in local politics. This seems like a desperate power struggle to me. We have no stake in this game. It's a lose-lose."

Riku thought silently for a moment. "We have no choice, Hiriko," Riku said. "I'd rather have one man die than fight a score of men on our way up the mountain."

"If we fail and we're captured, they'll execute us. And how do we know that just because Boss Kojiro dies, his men will throw down their arms and leave?"

Shin cut in, "They'll realize that they're no longer getting paid and they'll leave. These are ronin after all. Masterless samurai. Sell-swords."

"Some ronin have *some* sense of honor and won't abandon their post so easily," Hiriko said.

"You're too optimistic," Shin said. "These ronin's sense of honor is only as thick as the pile of gold placed in their palms."

Hiriko fell silent and thought it over. He went to face the window and looked out over the sea. He felt the cool breeze on his face. The sun was on its way down in the west. *What could one local mission hurt? I've been up against deadlier odds.* Without looking at them, he took a deep breath in and a deep breath out and said, "Alright. I'll agree to it, but I don't like it."

After a pause, Shin cracked a smile and said, "Very good. Here is the map of the castle given to me by the Daimyo himself." He placed it over the map of Opporo.

Chapter 20

Heartbeat

The setting sun painted the sky pink and orange. Kwan's stomach woke her up from her nap. *I suppose I should pay Gung Lao a visit.* Her orange flower print black robes sat at her feet folded neatly. She rolled out of bed and put the robes on, then massaged her stomach. Tiger Claw rested in its sheath next to where she lay. She strapped it to her waist. As she left her room, she closed the door behind her and saw an old woman leave her own bedroom. They locked eyes and that was when Kwan recognized her.

"Hey, you are the woman we met on the road!" Kwan said surprised.

The old woman grinned. "Indeed I am, young one."

"If you don't mind my asking, how did you arrive here so quickly? I thought you were headed in the opposite direction?"

The old woman didn't answer and chuckled. "Where is your companion? I thought you two were traveling together."

"We were, but he fell ill. We came to rest here in Omamori."

The old woman gave a knowing nod. "It was that man Iito, wasn't it? Curse his name."

"How did you know that?" Kwan asked, surprised.

"Word has spread of a demon roaming the lands with that name. No one knows what he's looking for, only that he'll punish anyone who crosses his path. Come now my child. Share a cup of tea with me downstairs." She turned her back and when she did not hear the creaky sounds of Kwan's footsteps atop the floorboards, she looked over her shoulder and beckoned her. Kwan scurried to catch up and followed her down into the common room. They sat down on the zabuton cushions. Kwan asked for two cups of tea, one for each of them.

The barkeeper asked, "Another glass of shochu for you miss?"

Kwan waved her off, embarrassed. She did not want to appear a lush in front of the old woman. "No. Just two cups of tea, thank you." The old woman seemed concerned but said nothing.

They settled in and waited for their tea. Some villagers came to *The Uchi Mata Inn* to get some relief after their long day's work, but none bothered them. Kwan felt an aura of warmth coming from the old woman and she remembered that she felt the same way the last time they met. It was a refreshing feeling compared to the constant cold she felt everywhere else in Omamori. Before long, the barkeeper came with a pot of hot tea and a portable coal burner to set it on. She also placed two porcelain teacups before the burner. She turned a knob and a wick of flame heated the bottom of the teapot.

"I recall you said something last we met," Kwan said. "You said the Great Tigress eternally chases the Spirit Dragon that stole her lover."

"Indeed, that is the story, young one," the old woman replied. Kwan filled the old woman's teacup, then her own before she placed the teakettle back on the burner.

"But one day the Great Tigress catches the Spirit Dragon. And you said, once her quest is complete…she dies…"

The old woman took a sip of the tea. "No, she will not die, young one. Spirits never die. She will move on to the Great Beyond, a realm none of us truly understand." She took another sip.

Kwan, who had not yet touched her tea, pensively peered into the cup. The leaves and foam gently swirled. She slowly brought the teacup to her lips and took a sip.

"To rescue her lover… it is her destiny," the old woman said with a graven face. Her body tensed. The old woman stared deeply into her eyes. "It is something she must do. She must go to the ends of the earth, to the deepest valleys, to the highest peaks, by any means necessary. Even if it takes an eternity, she must do it. It is her destiny."

Kwan felt a sinking feeling in the pit of her stomach, her hands trembled and her breath quickened. The old woman would not break her eye contact. It felt as if she was inside her head, reading her thoughts. A voice whispered inside her head, *The day will come soon. Be ready.*

"What did you say!?" Kwan exclaimed.

The old woman broke her eye contact for a moment. She looked down at her tea, then back at her. "I said it is the Tigress' destiny. Death comes for us all one day. It is best to spend our time wisely." Kwan looked to the window of the common room and noticed the sun had gone down. It was too dark to visit Gung Lao. She looked back over to the old woman who smiled a warmly comforting smile. She felt Tiger Claw gently pulse at her waist as if it had a heartbeat.

The barkeeper came over to their table. Kwan asked her to wake her up at sunrise, to which the barkeeper promised.

"You are a mighty warrior, I can tell," the old woman said. "That sword you carry, it does not look ordinary." Kwan untied the strap and held it horizontally before the old woman. Its pulse thickened. Kwan pulled the blade out just enough to show the engravement. The three claw marks glimmered in an orange luster. The old woman covered Kwan's hand that held the handle. She gently guided the blade back into the sheath.

She said, "This is a sacred sword. The way it pulses means it is alive. This is Tiger Claw, is it not?"

There was something about the old woman that she trusted, as if she had known her for her entire life. Speaking to her was like interacting with her own mother. "It is," Kwan admitted.

"And when it was given to you, did you plunge it into your belly?"

"No, I simply held it."

"Then you are the one that was truly meant to carry it. Listen to the sword. It will guide you through your true path. The sword belongs to you, and you to it. You will never know a more reliable ally." Kwan sat dumbfounded and when she came to her senses she strapped it to her waist. The old woman finished the last of her teacup. She stood and put her hand on Kwan's shoulder. Kwan felt a feeling of stillness and warmth travel from her shoulder to her heart. Without another word the old woman walked up the stairs, although they did not creak. Soon after, Kwan finished her tea and made her way upstairs and down the hall to her own room. She took off her robes and set Tiger Claw against the side of her bed. Then, she laid down on the soft bed and fell asleep. She listened to Tiger Claw's slow, warm heartbeat until she lost consciousness.

"Miss, the sun is 'bout to rise," the barkeeper said. Kwan rubbed the sleep out of her eyes. She reached over for Tiger Claw and there it was. It leaned against the bed right where she left it.

"Thank you. I'll be checking out."

"Alright. Y'can pay at the counter. I hope you enjoyed yer stay." Kwan smiled at her as she sat up and the barkeeper closed the door behind her. She put her robes on and gathered her things. She strapped Tiger Claw to her waist on her way down the stairs. Once in the common room she walked to the bar.

"I'll cover the old woman's tab as well," Kwan said to the barkeeper.

The barkeeper seemed confused. "What ol' woman?"

Equally as puzzled, Kwan said, "The old woman I shared tea with last night. You served us tea." The barkeeper did not seem any less confused.

"I only recall y'rself drinking tea. You were examining yer sword. I did think it curious how y'ordered two teacups just for yerself."

"You mean you didn't see an old woman?" The barkeeper shook her head blankly. "Okay, then I'll pay just my costs then."

She handed over the appropriate coin and wandered out of *The Uchi Mata Inn.*

It was a clear, chilly day. The sun had yet to rise. *Should I visit Gung Lao one last time? I don't want to miss* The Blue Shogun *again. He'll have to recover on his own.* She entered the crowded road and made her way to the harbor. As she approached it, her heartbeat quickened. *Oh, Spirits please don't let me miss it again. Let it be there. Please let it be there.* And there it was. The wooden seacraft rested at the docks. She hurried to the on-ramp and handed the crewman her fare. She gave a sigh of relief as the sailor ushered her aboard. She found a bench on the port side and sat down. There was some smelly residue on the railing next to her as if someone vomited there. She cringed and slid down the bench a few feet. She looked over the starboard side and watched as the sun peeked over the oceanic horizon. She couldn't remember the last time she left Honshu, if she ever had. All she knew about Hokkaido was that it was cold. *Riku went to the island and that's my destination too. I must reach the shrine atop Hokkenzen Mountain before he does. There is no other option.*

Chapter 21

The Castle

Shin and the others diverged off the main road an hour ago. There was only the barest hint of a footpath through the foliage. The entrance to the secret passage into Opporo Castle was nothing if not hidden. It was cold in the forests of Hokkaido this time of year. They trudged through fresh snow up to their ankles. Shin led the way followed by Riku and then Hiriko with Kasume taking up the rear. He hacked at the foliage that blocked their path while Hiriko looked around warily, still mistrustful of Shin. Kasume shivered and clutched his arms to his chest.

"Are we close?" Kasume asked while his lower lip trembled from the cold.

"Here we are," Shin said. They approached what looked like little more than a mound of loosely packed shrubbery covered in a thin layer of snow. The thief reached into the mound and with effort pulled open a trapdoor. The door itself was covered in planted grass, sticks, and leaves as if it hadn't been touched in decades. "This is it. Our way in."

Kasume's eyes widened. Hiriko said, "I don't see the city walls anywhere. Are you sure this is it?"

"Always the skeptic, young man," Shin said. "Yes this is it. I said it was well hidden, did I not? This underground passage is two miles long and lets out directly inside the castle behind the stables."

Riku said, "The plan is to take the passage and emerge after dusk. Then we can carry out the assassination."

Hiriko took Riku aside, "Riku-san, I don't like this. This seems too risky with too little in it for us. It is not too late to turn back."

Riku contemplated, then said, "I understand your concern Hiriko-kun. But our plan is very straight forward. We go in, kill Boss Kojiro, and get out. Then our path to the shrine will be cleared." He patted Hiriko on the shoulder and gave a reassuring smile. "I'll make sure we're safe." Hiriko did not return the smile.

From the entrance as he held open the door, Shin said, "Are we ready?" They peered into the passage. The rotted wooden steps led down into a single-file corridor just high enough for a full-grown man to stand upright. The darkness was impenetrable.

Riku said, "Let's go." Shin led the way down into the dark passage. They went in single file in the same order.

It was cool in the passage, but there was an absence of snow, which gave them some relief. Hiriko could not bring himself to take his hand off the handle of his sword at his hip. It was the deepest darkness Hiriko had ever experienced, even darker than the cave of the swords. At least then they had torches. It took some time, but his eyes adjusted enough to see Riku's figure in front of him.

They walked for what felt to Hiriko like an eternity. *It's a trap. Guards are waiting for us. They're going to kill us, torture us first. I never should've agreed to this.* Lost in thought, he found himself forgetting where he was. There was nothing but endless trudging through frigid, disorienting darkness. He shook himself to the present again and again in attempts to fend off his nervous thoughts.

Finally, from ahead Shin said, "We're nearly there. Here, the end." A sliver of moonlight poured through from the top of the stairway. It was a more than welcome sight. "Good, it's already after dark."

"Stick to the plan," Riku said. "We go in, kill the ronin boss, and leave the way we came. Don't make a sound."

Shin listened to the noises that came from above the trapdoor. When he heard nothing he lifted it up a smidge and peeked. When the coast was clear he lifted the door over onto the ground and the ninjas snuck out. It was refreshing to be out of the darkness of the tunnel. But they could not relish the feeling for long. The trap door let out behind the stables in the castle courtyard, just as Shin said. The covered open-air wooden stables held several horses and provided only partial visual cover for the trapdoor, so they had to move quickly.

Just like on the map, there was a shack against the inside of the stone-gray castle walls. It had a low-hanging black shingle roof. The group of them ran as fast as they could next to the wall until they reached the shack. They quickly ran up the wall onto its roof. Far ahead, further along the curved stone castle walls was the pagoda, the keep of the castle where the ronin boss slept. Shin took out his rope and grappling hook and flung it up over the castle wall battlement. The hook caught. He gave the rope a few test tugs then he and the ninjas, one by one, scaled the castle wall. When the last of them, Kasume, climbed over the battlement, they snuck along the castle wall's walkway. Hiriko found it suspicious that there were no guards to deal with along the way.

They reached the keep. It was a layered pagoda building several stories tall. Even in the moonlight its white walls and black tiled rooves stacked in layers looked impressive. They saw guards far below unaware of them. There was a gap from the castle wall to the nearest roof of the pagoda. One by one they leapt across. Each landed silently. The moon above provided their only source of light. Shin slid open the window and they snuck into the second level of the pagoda.

The hallways were barren with white *shoji* doors and paneling that separated individual rooms on both sides of the wooden floored hallway. They needed to silently sneak up two floors and into Boss Kojiro's bedroom. To be sure of the location, Riku pulled out the map and checked the layout. The stairs lay at the far end of the hallway. They crept, silent as night. They heard the snores of ronin guards as they tip-toed past. They reached the wooden staircase and climbed as silently as they could up two flights to the fourth floor. Now they were on the same floor as their target. The ninjas took out their ninjato swords. Shin fell back and Riku took the lead. They inched forward, closer and closer to Boss Kojiro's bedroom. They reached it. Riku gripped the edge of the shoji door. From behind him, Kasume gave a gasp. Riku turned and saw Shin hold Kasume from behind with a knife to his throat. Boss Kojiro's shoji flung open and revealed several ronin, swords drawn. The door on the opposite side opened too with several more ronin and their blades at the ready. Kasume struggled and pulled at the arm around his neck.

"Shin! You traitor!" Riku exclaimed.

Shin chuckled and said, "I can't believe you didn't recognize me, Riku." With his free hand, Shin rubbed his face and revealed his true identity. "My master has been eager to meet with you." It was the Ghost of Shō himself, Iito.

Riku was slack-jawed. Hiriko shook his head and said, "I knew this was a trap from the beginning." Kasume breathed hard and his face turned red. The swordsmen on both sides stepped closer and tightened their surround.

Hiriko looked to Riku and said, "What do we do?"

Iito said, "There's nothing you can do except surrender." Kasume struggled hard but Iito held him firmly.

Riku closed his eyes and centered himself. Deep breath in, deep breath out. Within the darkest recesses of his mind a drop of dew slid down a gray leaf. The droplet clung to the end of the leaf until it fell into a pool of still water below. The ripples were clear but soon glowed a luminescent violet. He opened his eyes. The world around him moved in slow motion. Hiriko's anxious face looked at him. The ronin on either side stood steadfast. And over Hiriko's shoulder Iito held Kasume. Riku put his hand in front of his eyes. Subtly, it glowed the same luminescent violet.

I'm here, Riku a booming voice said to him from within his mind. And Riku knew who it was. It was the spirit dragon, *Noroi no Owari*.

"Get down," Riku calmly whispered to Hiriko.

Riku reeled his glowing hand back and with all his might struck at the space in front of him. Strong winds blasted through the walls of the pagoda from behind Riku. It tore them to shrapnel and opened the entire level as if there were no walls

186

there to begin with. Only the support beams were left. The winds carried the ronin off their feet and out of the far end of the now open-air building to their deaths below. Of the enemy, only Iito kept his footing and still held onto Kasume. The walls of the fourth floor of the pagoda gave way to a panoramic view of the night sky. The carnage visibly shook Iito. Kasume seized the moment. He grabbed Iito's arm, lowered his own hips and tossed Iito over himself onto the ground. Then he dashed to Riku and Hiriko. Iito picked himself up.

With the younger ninjas behind him, Riku reeled back again and struck forth with his palm. Iito tried to lean into the wind, but it was too strong and it threw him to the edge of the building. He looked behind himself. It was a sheer drop.

One last time Riku forced the air forward. The wind flooded forth in the form of a transparent, violet dragon. The ephemeral beast was enormous and it filled the room as it coiled from one side to the other with its blinding, illuminating luster. It swooped over to Iito, gripped him in its jaws, and carried him off his feet over the edge of the building and out of sight.

Riku breathed hard. The illumination around his arm faded and he collapsed to his knees. Kasume and Hiriko rushed to his aid.

"C'mon Riku," Hiriko said. "We gotta get out of here."

Weakly, Riku replied, "I should've trusted your intuition, Hiriko. It was a trap, just like you said. I was wrong. There probably aren't even any guards on the path. I'm a fool."

Hiriko could not help but crack a smirk. "Let's just get out of here. Can you make it?"

Kasume looked over the edge and said, "We can make it if we dive into the moat below."

Riku smiled and said, "Four stories up? No problem." Though exhausted, he was able to stand. They heard rumblings of men making their way up the stairs.

"Then let's go," Hiriko said. One by one they took a running start and jumped out of the building over the castle wall and into the waters of the moat four stories below. The ronin guards found only an empty, open-air room.

Chapter 22

Sleep

The three ninjas climbed out of the moat and did not stop until they made it deep into the cover of the trees. Once they believed they were safe, they laid down on their backs. They were exhausted and wet and their robes were muddied and frozen.

"It seems the demon lord has already gathered followers in Opporo," Riku said.

"It seems so," said Hiriko.

Riku rummaged around in his pocket and felt for it. It was the bone scroll the old couple had given to him on the passage to Hokkaido.

"I'm exhausted," said Kasume. "Maybe we can find some place to stay."

"Remember that merchant on the boat?" Riku asked. "His name was Gishi. He told me there are hot springs on the outskirts of Opporo. Those usually have an inn attached. Perhaps we can find it and stay there."

"A warm bed sounds lovely," Kasume replied, his lower jaw trembled from the cold. He was pale and felt miserable from the water that padded his clothes. "It feels like I've been freezing for as long as I can remember. I can't wait to feel warm again."

"Not to say, 'I told you so,' but, Shin was suspicious from the beginning." Hiriko said.

"That's the last time I trust a thief," Riku said.

"How did we not recognize Iito! I feel like a fool," Kasume said.

"He had an illusory mask on his face," Riku said. "It made him look like someone else until he revealed himself. It's an old, forbidden ninjutsu technique. We should expect our enemies to use every trick in existence against us. Kasume, are you okay? Are you hurt?"

"No, just a little rattled. And frozen," he replied. "The sooner we make it out of here the better. Speaking of which, are you both ready? I'm cold."

"We're far enough removed that we can build a fire," Hiriko said. "I'll gather some dry firewood. You two stay here." Hiriko got up and brushed the loose dirt and snow off his robes, though despite this, he was still covered in dried mud. He left them to gather the firewood.

Riku's arms were too heavy to lift and he soon lost consciousness. Kasume began mumbling to himself before he too fell asleep. When Hiriko returned carrying a bundle of firewood he saw his companions passed out.

"So irresponsible. They didn't even leave someone on guard duty. I guess that means I'm it." Hiriko dropped the firewood carelessly on the ground next to them. He crouched and rearranged them into a proper pile, then took out his piece of flint and sparked the fire. The flames quickly caught and he was left with a modest campfire.

The moonlight that reflected off the snow made visibility slightly better. Hiriko poked around at the fire with a long stick early into the morning while his companions slept.

I really should've stood up for myself. And it turned out I was right; it was a trap all along. See Hiriko? Trust your instincts. Be a man. Don't let anyone sway your resolve. Spirits, Iito really frightened me. I hope that'll be the last we see of him. The spirit dragon, Noroi no Owari. *He's so powerful. But is he powerful enough to stand up to the demon lord? I certainly hope so.*

Helplessness. Spirits, I had never felt so helpless before in my life. There had to be twenty, no, thirty ronin ready to chop us to pieces. Riku-sensei and the dragon saved us. I had never seen him use that power before. Back at the temple, the dragon spewed holy fire. But it has the power of wind too? What more can this dragon do?

Hiriko poked at the fire again as he lost himself in his thoughts. He heard footsteps behind him but he did not feel alarmed nor concerned.

"What's troubling you, young one?" an old man said from behind him. "And can I share this fire with you? It's quite chilly."

"Yes of course you can share the fire," Hiriko said. "Be my guest." The thought crossed his mind to rouse the others but he decided there was little point. He looked up through the trees and saw the stars twinkling in the midnight skies above.

"What's troubling you, and what's your name young man?"

The old man had a warm aura about him. He exuded a pleasing flowery aroma as well. Hiriko felt he could trust him. "Hiriko. My name is Hiriko," he said. "My companions and I were just lured into a trap. We were in such deep trouble that it took a miracle from the Spirits to get us out of it. We're lucky to be alive."

191

"I see. So, you've been through a lot. What's next?"

Hesitantly, Hiriko said, "Well, we keep carrying on, I suppose."

"That's right young man. You keep carrying on." The old man comfortingly placed his hand on Hiriko's shoulder. He instantly felt a warm sensation take over him and he felt incredibly sleepy. Hiriko found himself lying down onto the ground and fell unconscious into a deep sleep.

A moment later, Riku blinked awake and saw the old man picking at the fire with Hiriko's stick.

"Who are you?" Riku asked concerned. The old man didn't answer. But Riku felt he knew who it was. He sat up across the fire from him. "You saved us."

The old man looked up from the fire to Riku, the wisps of the orange flame crackling between them. "The demons lured you into a trap. You summoned me, so it was you who saved yourself."

Riku said nothing for a moment and stared into the fire. Then he said, "Now what?"

More silence. The old man scratched his chin and said, "You will soon be tested. You will have a choice to make, and I can't make that choice for you." Riku looked through the fire at the old man's stick. The flames of the fire furled and fuzzed the air. Riku's view of the stick blurred and he soon realized it was more than just a stick, it was a sword.

"Is that—? Riku asked.

"Yes," he said. "I have come to return Dragon Fang to its rightful keeper." They each stood and the old man met Riku halfway around the fire. The elder presented Riku with the sword in its sheath. He pulled it out just enough to reveal the engravement. Riku looked closely and saw the dragon that breathed a puff of fire. He took the sword and bowed.

"Now you have everything you need. The sword and the scroll both."

"The scroll?" He felt for the bone scroll in his pocket. The old couple on the ship meant for him to have it. But who were they really? Riku had a sudden suspicion that he had been watched the entire journey, by enemies and friends alike. He pulled out the scroll and examined its markings closely. The markings still seemed unintelligible to him. "What do the markings say?" he asked.

"They indicate that you will have a choice. No one can make the choice but you. You must choose between the one you once loved, or the one whose fate is tied with that of the world. When you are ready, climb the mountain. Only there can you make the choice. But go alone."

Riku fell silent. "A choice? I don't understand. I have so many questions. I don't even know where to begin," Riku said.

"In time all will be revealed," the old man said. "Now, go back to sleep. You will need your strength for the journey ahead." The old man put his hand on Riku's shoulder. A comfortable sleepiness overtook him. He sat down and fell over asleep. The old man sat back down and stared into the fire.

Deep in his dream, Riku felt cold, but not just the cold he was used to. No, he felt it in his bones. He found himself alone hiking along a rocky frozen mountain ridge. The air battered him from both sides and it felt as if he wore no weather protection at all though he was wrapped head to toe. The wind carried powdery snow that intermittently obscured his view.

The peak was only a half mile away now. Between gusts of snow, he could make out a stone enclosure built into the mountainside just before the peak. It must be Hokkenzen Shrine. He was almost there! He was so excited that his foot slipped on the snow and he fell on his knee. He brushed himself off before he trekked on.

He took careful step after careful step. He was nearly there. As he approached, to his surprise, he saw fresh human tracks along the ridge. His chest rumbled and the hair stood up on the back of his neck. Instinctively he covered the handle of his sword with his hand.

Only a few paces from the stone enclosure, the tracks led to a woman that stood in the ankle-high snow. She faced the frozen shrine with her back to him. Her long dark hair swayed in the wind. She wore black robes with orange flower print that were unsuited for the conditions, though she stood like a stone. As Riku approached, his foot crunched the snow underfoot and the woman quickly looked over her shoulder at him. She wore a mask with the visage of a tiger baring its fangs.

He woke up and gasped for breath with the image of the woman in the mask stuck in his mind. He found himself at their makeshift campsite. The fiery embers smoldered. Hiriko and Kasume slept soundly. He felt for a sword on his belt and Dragon Fang was there. He gave a sigh of relief, though he took heavy breaths. It was early morning and sunbeams snuck their ways through the trees.

Who was that woman at the shrine? Why was she there?
Was she waiting for me? I have so many unanswered questions.

/ / /

When Yenfay beat her at archery, Mizu refused to let it go.
Every spare moment she had, she shot arrows. From close and
from far she shot them. When she broke her bow, Akari let her
use hers, but she broke that one too. After Daisuke-sensei
scolded them he gave each of them a new one. But she broke
them. After a scolding from Minato-sama this time, they were
each given stronger bows. Even Mizu could not break them.

Akari's job had been to fetch the bundle of arrows from the
target tree. Each time, she tried to get there and back faster than
the last run. Mizu would count how long she took. *Ichi, ni, san,
shi.* When Akari grew bored, she would flip as she ran. The next
run she would increase it to two. Before long she would do flips
all the way there and all the way back. Then she did the same
with backflips.

Mizu made retrieving the arrows easy for Akari. After a few
weeks of practice, Mizu stopped missing the target. Be it a
windy day or a clear day, her arrows refused to miss. She made
herself dizzy spinning in circles, but she still hit the target.
Moving targets were tricky, but soon Daisuke-sensei became
upset with how many dead rabbits they brought back. Akari shot
sometimes to keep her skills sharp and she became good too.
Mizu was a good instructor.

Grandmaster Minato taught the girls the tea ceremony. He
and Mikoto showed them everything from what to wear and

where to sit, to the different bowls to use and how hot to make the water; every fragment of etiquette. Akari found sitting still on her knees on the tatami floor for just that short amount of time harder than archery, but she did not fuss or complain. After many failed tries, Akari performed the entire ceremony on her own with no mistakes and she shared her tea with Mizu.

During ninjutsu practice in the courtyard, Daisuke-sensei made a point to pair Akari with the toughest boys. He reasoned that if she could outlast the training, her throwing technique would be flawless.

"Akari-kun, load him onto one leg, then sweep it," he told her from the sidelines. Yasu was a foot taller than her. She held the bigger boy by the arm and lapel of his *gi* and shifted him onto one leg. But as hard as she tried, his leg wouldn't budge. "When he's on the one leg, push through him, then sweep. Try that!" Daisuke-sensei called. She tried again, but Yasu still wouldn't budge.

"You can do it Akari!" Mizu said while entangled with her own partner.

Akari grew frustrated. She grabbed Yasu's arm and lapel, and as she loaded his weight onto one leg, she smashed her shoulder into his, pushed through, and at the same time swept the leg. The boy tumbled back. "I did it!"

"You did it exactly right, Akari!" Daisuke said. "Your technique must be correct each time for it to work on someone bigger than you. Now! Ninety-nine more times. Go!" Akari groaned. She looked over at the black belts. They were performing throws that sent their opponents flying. But the one that was thrown just dusted himself off and went at it again.

Daisuke noticed her looking at them and saw the worry in her eyes. He ran to her side. "It helps to know how to fall," he said. "Soon you'll test for yellow belt. I can't believe how skilled you and Mizu have become. Always challenge yourselves but don't be afraid to fall. Falling is the first part of getting back up. And every time we get back up, we get stronger. Before long, you'll get up so many times that no one can stop you. Not even a demon."

Akari stared up at Daisuke-sensei and thought over what he said. She remembered that night, the crushed flower, the demon of black flames, and the flight for her life. Chills ran down her spine. *One day, when I become strong enough, not even a demon can stop me. It'll be the* demons *that run from* me. She looked over to Yasu. She said to him, "Let's go again Yasu. Ninety-nine more times."

Chapter 23

Guide

Kwan felt more revitalized than ever. She finally made it to Hakazu, the port town of Hokkaido Island. She was going to catch Riku, defeat him, and bring back Unomichi. Although, she still was not quite sure how she was going to do that. *Once I catch up to him, he'll tell me with his dying breath how to bring him back to life. That's the bottom line.*

She left the docks at a quick pace. Tiger Claw had not rumbled during the passage across the channel but she covered its handle just the same. The townspeople she passed by had an odd accent she was unused to, though she could understand them just fine. They seemed to gossip about something that made quite a stir. She caught a few stray words like *Opporo* and *castle* and something about a dragon. It could mean Riku had made it there and caused trouble.

Oh, that blasted Koga. Just stay in one place already so I can make you pay for what you've done.

"Excuse me, miss," she asked a passerby, "Do you know the way to Opporo?"

"Opporo?" the young woman replied in her accent. "Why? Do you want to catch the dragon yourself?"

"What do you mean?"

"You mean you haven't heard? The castle of Opporo was attacked! The pagoda was nearly destroyed! You should stay away from there." She walked off before Kwan could ask her any more questions.

She approached another young woman. "Excuse me, do you know how to get to Opporo?" The girl just shook her head and kept walking as if she felt insulted. *Can't they see that this is important?* She asked a few more people, and each gave her a judgmental glance before they ignored her and went about their business. *It's no use. No one will help me.*

"You're looking to go to Opporo?" a man said from behind her. He was tall and thin and wore a whicker round brimmed hat and dark green robes. He obscured something beneath his robes, probably a short walking stick. "Good luck with that. Yesterday they closed all the roads that lead to the city. The closures will last at least a month."

Kwan tightened her fists and pouted. She thought for a moment. *If Riku made a scene at Opporo, then he's already left and is on his way up the mountain! Maybe he's already at the top!*

"Excuse me," she asked the man as a boiling frustration simmered beneath her voice, "but you wouldn't know a way up Hokkenzen Mountain, would you?"

The man touched his chin and thought for a moment before replying, "Well, the easiest way is the mountain trail from Opporo. But, with that not being an option... Let's see... You could try crossing the bay on a small boat. But wait, that won't work. Then you'd have to climb cliffs. Hmm..." The man mumbled to himself for a moment and thought it over. Kwan looked around impatiently.

Someone tapped Kwan on the shoulder. She looked to see who it was and found another man sporting a weathered backpack that had seen better days. "I can get you on the trail," he said. Kwan's face lit up. He was handsome with short dark hair and a sharp jaw, and he looked fit to boot. "I don't do it for free though."

"What do you mean you can get me on the trail?" she asked.

"I know the natural layout of this island better than anyone. I'm a climber, hiker, and survivalist. And for you, I'll be your guide." He took her hand and kissed her knuckle before he looked up with a smile. Kwan cracked a smile before she snatched her hand back.

The first man groaned. "Hanzo-san. Always the scoundrel. But what he says is true, if anyone can get you onto the path, he can."

Kwan look from one man to the other before she reluctantly agreed. She noticed Hanzo carried a *katana* of a samurai as well as a *tanto* short sword. The katana's handle, once white, was now browned with sweat and dirt. The tanto's handle was less so, but both needed attention.

"Are you a samurai?" Kwan asked.

"Yes, we both are," Hanzo said. "Where're your swords, Shogo-san?"

"Right here," Shogo said. He unveiled a pair of samurai swords attached to his hip from under his sage green robes. "Can't be caught without them." His showed a little wear but seemed to fare better than Hanzo's.

"I've sort of... fallen on hard times," Hanzo said.

"You mean you bet your house and lost," Shogo taunted.

"Right... But it's water under the bridge."

"Water under the bridge?" Shogo scoffed. "You're on the streets! You nearly lost your status as a samurai. And I nearly lost mine for associating with you." Kwan's eyebrows raised the more she learned about this man, but she could not help but chuckle to herself.

"Forget all that," Hanzo said. "Anyways, that's why I'm earning some coin doing odd jobs like this. You can pay, right?"

Kwan half-smiled and said, "Yes I can pay."

"I know a way onto the path. But we'll have to do some climbing. Is that okay with you miss, erm, what was your name?"

"Kwan. My name is Kwan."

"Of course it is. To get to the path by dusk, we would need to leave here early in the morning. Is that an issue?"

Kwan thought back to the last time she had to be up early when she missed the boat to the island and set herself back an entire day. "No, that shouldn't be a problem. Although, I have no place to spend the night."

Shogo said, "I have plenty of room in my residence for guests. Please, you're welcome to occupy one of my spare rooms for the night."

Kwan bowed and said, "Thank you, that is very kind."

Hanzo began, "Good. It's settled. Now, there are docks on the opposite side of the peninsula to the north on the bay. We'll borrow a small rowboat and I'll take the lead from there. We'll leave at sunrise tomorrow morning. It's not too far. We need all the daylight we can get. If we leave now it'll be dark by the time we reach the docks. We must wait."

Shogo said, "Come. Let me show you to my home. My wife is very friendly."

/ / /

Zeshiro offered to handle the demons that were to come through the portal at Mount Kyokushin's peak. Naturally Aurabos would

201

be the one to tag along. Daisuke protested, but Grandmaster Minato wanted to use it as a test to prove their alliance.

As the silvery full moon approached the apex of the mountain peak Zeshiro tensed. He gripped his *tekko-kagi* claws firmly in each hand. Aurabos stood with his wind sword held stoically. The gusts were very strong at the mountain peak but the demons stood as still as stones. The clouds parted slowly. Nearly a minute left.

"I will leave your side soon, as you no longer possess Dragon Fang," Aurabos reminded.

"Isn't defeating the demon lord a little more important than guarding a blasted sword?" Zeshiro asked.

"I was created with a solitary purpose: to protect the swords of the cave. It is unfortunate enough that they were separated in the first place. You should not have given it up if you wished for my further protection."

"The sword spoke to me. It told me to give it back. I can't really explain it. It felt in all ways the right thing to do."

"Very well."

The last of the clouds parted away from the glowing moon. As it had many times before, a stripe like a brush stroke split the moon in two before them. Four ninjas clothed in white robes appeared. They each touched the ground as they gently landed crouched.

"Unexpected," Aura said. "There were to be only two. But four there are."

"Every Koga we've met said there are always two. Well, I'm not pausing to ask questions," Zeshiro snapped. The ninjas fanned out while the demons considered their predicament. They were quickly surrounded. Zeshiro surged forward towards one with an uppercut jab, but narrowly missed the nimble target. He punched and slashed with his claws but met only empty space each time. "A slippery one, are you?" The white-robed demon ninja from behind him swung his ninjato and nearly cut Zeshiro but he caught the sword in time between his claws. As he twisted the tekko-kagi, the ninja lost his grip and let go, now defenseless. Zeshiro launched the sword end over end until it struck the ninja hard where his shoulder met his neck. The ninja fell, lifeless. Zeshiro continued to engage the other white-robed ninja.

The other two pelted the stone-like Aurabos with quick strikes, though their blows bounced off harmlessly. As the attackers considered their next move, Aurabos wound up a heavy swing and let it loose. The swipe blew a gust so razor sharp that it cut both ninjas in half. It bisected their bodies at the waist. Behind him Zeshiro landed a critical uppercut blow on the last ninja. The ninja fell to the ground dead, a nasty wound that ran up his torso reflected his cause of death. They gathered the bodies together and set them ablaze with the matches they carried. The red flames glowed until they died down.

"Objective complete," said Aurabos. "Although, it was rather odd that there were four."

"Four. The number of the demon," Zeshiro said as he stared at the silvery full moon. The portal sealed itself. "Let us bring the remains of their heads as proof. This is not a good sign."

"Perhaps it is a message from the demon lord. A warning."

Zeshiro let a moment of silence pass. "There may be a plot brewing. We must warn the humans."

"Very well," Aurabos said. They gathered the burned remains and set off down the mountain path toward Koga Temple.

Daisuke and a small host of Koga ninjas were at the gate of Koga Temple. They turned as Grandmaster Minato approached from behind. He too waited at the gate. The full moon had obscured itself below the horizon. Before long, Zeshiro and Aurabos approached as they carried the heads of their victims.

They unloaded the blackened unrecognizable heads on the ground before the ninjas who had waited much of the night for their return.

"There were four," Zeshiro said.

The Grandmaster came forward. "Four. You say there were four. Usually there are two. Explain." Each Koga ninja held a countenance of strong concern. They looked to each other for some sort of explanation.

"I believe it to be a sign the demon lord's plans are brewing," Zeshiro said. "He is a master of strategy. This may have been a ploy to distract us or a stick to prod us. Either way, it is a reminder for us to stay vigilant. His plans are always long winded. Meddling here and there all the while his enemies defeat themselves."

Minato stiffened his jaw and said, "Thus, we must join with our allies. Strengthen our bonds. Daisuke-san, prepare a messenger to Iga Temple. They must be alerted at once."

"Right away," Daisuke nodded and started into the courtyard.

"You have done well, demons," Minato said. "You have gained our trust. Consider yourselves honorable allies of Koga Temple."

Zeshiro brought his fist to his heart and bowed. Aura nodded with respect.

Chapter 24

Climb

Riku opened his eyes. Hiriko and Kasume bantered about something while they roasted some freshly caught rabbits over their campfire.

"Oh, he's awake," Hiriko said. He and Kasume looked over at him from the logs they sat on.

Riku groggily said, "How long was I out for?"

"Well, it's nearly midday," Kasume said. "You seemed peaceful so we decided not to bother you. While you were asleep we caught something to eat. Here, we've roasted a rabbit for you." He handed him a skewered, blackened rabbit. He pulled off a bit of meat. To his surprise it did not taste entirely terrible, though it could have used some salt. The others tried theirs as well and were equally satisfied.

Their campfire site was on a rocky patch amongst a thick group of leafless trees.

"If we make it to the mountain path, perhaps we can stop in at the hot springs. There we can eat a proper meal and be well rested for the climb," Riku said. He took a big bite off the skewer.

"I did some scouting this morning," Hiriko said. "It looks like the hot springs you spoke of are not far away. Though I worry that warriors from Opporo Castle will be notified if we visit it."

"We'll be fine," Riku said.

"'We'll be fine?' Is that the best you can do?" Hiriko protested, hands on his hips.

"Hiriko, we'll die if we stay out in this cold for much longer. Either we risk capture, or we freeze to death." Riku said. Hiriko looked over to Kasume.

After a moment Kasume said, "That's good enough for me. It's freezing out here. I'm tired of being frozen." He bit into the meat.

The three of them finished their meal and doused the flames by throwing armfuls of snow onto it. They covered their tracks and made it appear as if they were never there.

They weaved their way silently between the barren trees toward the steam that came from the far side of the snowy hills. The trees were densely cropped and each one was rough to the touch, their bark irritated by the wet and the cold. The footing of the hills was slippery and Kasume found it difficult to make his way up unless he grasped the spiky bark. His nearly frostbitten hands gathered some scratches with each touch. But before long they reached the top of the furthest hill. Through the trees below they could see the source. The steam came from several natural hot springs at the base of the hill. There was a wooden building nearby, presumably the inn that serviced the hot springs.

"Oh finally!" Kasume said. He blew his breath into his shaking hands.

Riku began, "We'll need to get to the front of the inn so we can—hey Kasume!" The young ninja already staggered down the hillside toward the hot pools of water. He picked up speed and brushed up against the roughness of the bark. Finally at the bottom just before the water he slipped and made a huge splash when he landed in the hot spring. The men already in the pool laughed at the sight. But Kasume didn't care, he was just glad to finally be warm.

"Usually you take everything off *before* you get in the water, hm?" one of the old men said to Kasume.

Riku and Hiriko slowly and carefully made their way down the hill and approached the side of the spring. Even Riku couldn't help but reach down and feel the warmth of the water in his hands.

The innkeeper came running. He was a middle-aged man, very thin and scrawny, though he wore an ornate jade robe that sat wide on his shoulders making him appear imposing. "These springs are not free to the public," he said to them. "They're private. You'll need to show yourselves out before I alert guards."

"Apologies sir," Riku said gesturing for the innkeeper to remain calm. "Apologies for our crude entrance. I come here by the recommendation of my good friend Gishi."

The innkeeper was slightly taken aback, but then smiled, "Ahh so you're friends of Gishi! Maybe you're the ones who will finally pay the extravagant tab he accrued on his last visit."

Riku thought for a moment, slightly stunned, then said, "We would be happy to. He is a close friend after all. How much of a bill could one traveling merchant accrue anyways?" *That Gishi. If I ever see him again I'll make him pay me back ten-fold.*

"Splendid. Come inside to the inn. Meet me at the counter. Then we can find you private rooms and your own *onsen* to warm up and relax in."

"Very good," Riku said. He looked over his shoulder at Hiriko, who still held their dwindling coin stash in his coin purse. Hopefully they had enough.

Riku and Hiriko followed the innkeeper inside. The lobby was very neatly decorated with solid red tapestries draping the walls and some trees and plants in green pots here and there on the wooden floors and beams that held up the upper levels. The bill ended up not being too costly, and they had plenty of coin left over after the transaction. Hiriko was itching to join Kasume in the hot springs. After they paid, the two of them went back outside over to the hot spring Kasume had fallen into. They found him still with all his clothes on. They beckoned him to come with them to their own private hot spring. He reluctantly agreed, though he didn't want to be out of the hot water even for a moment. The innkeeper guided them to their hot spring pool. This time they shed their clothes and dipped themselves in. It was comfortable enough to make the three of them drowsy. The steam had a pleasant aroma that numbed their senses. It was perfect here: the warmth, the beautiful scenery, everything. Riku had not felt this relaxed in ages. His mind drifted.

I'm sorry Unomichi. I'm sorry you died. Truly. But I can't miss this opportunity to bring back Yuuki-chan. I don't care what Grandmaster will say. I don't care if I'm punished. I need her back here with me. I hope you can forgive me.

/ / /

A harsh knock on her door woke her up. "Miss Kwan, it's sunrise. It's time to get ready." Kwan groggily looked over at the one who woke her and saw the tall samurai peek into her room.

"Thank you Shogo-san," she said with a cracked voice. She stretched and sat up off the bed roll on which she laid. This could be the last real bed she slept on for a while.

She put on her black robes with orange flower print and strapped Tiger Claw to her hip. When she put it on, it started to rumble and pulse uncontrollably. She squeezed the handle with her palm and it seemed to calm some, but not entirely. It was concerning but she didn't know how else to soothe it.

"Anything wrong, Kwan-san?" Shogo asked, oblivious to the sword's grief.

"No, everything's fine, thank you." She went with him to the dining room where they met with Hanzo and enjoyed a quaint meal of eggs over rice and some herbal tea.

"I'll accompany you as far as the docks on the north side of the peninsula," Shogo said. "Then I'll say my goodbyes."

"I'll take you across the bay until we reach the path. There will be some climbing. Hopefully you're prepared for that," Hanzo said.

Kwan gave a sideways smile. "I'm a ninja of the Iga clan. I'm more than prepared."

Hanzo smiled at her response. "Very good," he said. "Then let's finish and get going."

The trio left Shogo's modest home and they followed the dusty footpath that led them north through the molting trees. As they ventured further up the path the trees became noticeably more leafless. There was a gentle fog obscuring their vision so not even the great mountains in the distance were visible.

Before long the path emptied out to the untouched sandy beach of the bay. At the water's edge there was a shoddy wooden pier that extended into the water for several yards and there were three rowboats on the beach.

"Good. I was worried the rowboats would be taken," Hanzo said. "Then we'd have to take a far hike around the bay. But we're lucky."

"This is where I leave you," Shogo said. "Be careful on your trek up the mountain path. It's a long way up. Be sure to rest along the way."

"I will. Thank you for your hospitality," Kwan said to him. They bowed to each other. She looked across the water and could just barely make out the cliffs on the far side. She swallowed hard. The distance across the bay was further than she anticipated. She jolted to her senses when Hanzo threw his climbing ropes into one of the rowboats with a loud *clunk*. The rowboat sat in the untouched sand at the water's edge, the slow rolling of the gentle waves did its best to pull in the tiny craft. The only thing that held it to shore was its immense weight and a loose rope that secured it to the base of the dilapidated pier. The pier, if one could call it that, was nothing more than a shaky metal frame with half-rotten wooden boards lined side by side comprising the deck. The boards were not even wide enough for two people to walk abreast.

Hanzo found only two oars amongst all the boats. He shrugged and quipped that at least no one could follow them. An unease tingled Kwan's spine at the thought of someone like Iito chasing after them in one of the other rowboats. She tried to shake the thought. The two of them shoved their chosen rowboat into the water and hopped in before it left them behind. The samurai assumed the rowing seat, his back to the direction of travel. Kwan sat facing Hanzo at the stern of the little wooden boat. Hanzo began to row. She looked over her shoulder at Shogo who saw them off. He grew smaller and smaller as they rowed further away. She turned back to Hanzo who was already in the throes of rowing. He gave her a smile with his square jaw and short facial hair, but she did not know how to handle the gesture, so she glanced down to the deepening blue water and gave him a grin. She thought he was handsome in a rugged sort of way. Maybe in another life they would have been together. Thoughts of them embracing and kissing crossed her mind but she tried to shake them. To her, no one could compete with Unomichi. He was the reason for her journey and she would not forsake him. Not in this life.

The waters of the bay were calm this time of day. The sunshine rays peeked through the clouds now and again, to varying success. Hanzo's breath became visible in the cold but she could not see her own. It felt to her like a warm spring day. She felt Tiger Claw at her hip rumble as strongly as ever. The handle felt warm. She became lost in thought as she held the sword to her chest and gazed at the waters over Hanzo's shoulder. *Are you trying to tell me something, Tiger Claw? Your rumbles have grown stronger and more frequent. What will I see once I reach the peak of the mountain? The thought of confronting him gives me chills, though you radiate such warmth. Soon I'll be reunited with my love. There must be a way to see him again.* The rowboat rocked and bumped and a few blinding sunbeams found their way through the clouds, though only for a moment. They took their few seconds to dance across the surface waters of the bay. Kwan glanced up at the silver linings of the clouds before the openings vanished.

Hanzo shivered more, between huffs and puffs, the further north he rowed them. The distant cliffs on the far side of the bay drew closer. It had only been an hour but already they neared their destination.

Finally, they reached the cliffside. The water level reached right up to the bare stone. It was a rocky wall fifty feet up to the grassy shelf above. Kwan's eyes dilated. "We're going to scale that?"

Hanzo grinned, "There is a ladder built into the cliffside that reaches to the shelf above. It's somewhere along the wall. A bit further down." He paused rowing for a moment to relax his shoulders. Then he steered the rowboat along the rocks. A layer of azure, translucent water swirled atop the murk of the seaweed green depths below. On the rocky cliffside, stacked layers of green damp moss reminded of the rise and fall of the tide. Before long they found their way to the ladder. It was a series of metal rungs hammered into the wall that scaled the cliffside all the way up. The rungs began below the water. The lowest ones below the tide and a few above were green with loose, soft moss.

"After you," Hanzo said. Kwan tightened her jaw and put on a brave face. From the rocking rowboat she touched the first rung. It was cold as ice and wet, yet it held firm. She stepped onto the ladder and began to climb rung by rung. "Just make sure not to look down." Hanzo fastened the rowboat to a low rung with a rope and lifted the oars and placed one end under the seat. Once he was satisfied, he rubbed his hands together and stretched his exhausted shoulders. He shifted his weight off the rowboat and onto the ladder. He would somehow have to find the strength to scale the many rungs.

The boat clunked around below them as the waves gently tossed it around. Kwan tried to put everything beneath her out of her mind as she climbed the rungs. The breeze threatened to chill her, but she still felt warm. There was nothing for her to look at except the rocky wall an inch from her face, and sky. A few times she caught herself glancing down to the deep waters below and regretted it each time. They were very high up now.

Finally, she reached the grassy shelf. She rolled onto the damp grass and breathed heavily. Shortly following, Hanzo reached the top and, like her, rolled onto the shelf exhausted.

Chapter 25

Reaching

Even though they were closer to the heavens, the sky was darker up here as the sun set below the cloud line. The vermillion and salmon colors were so beautiful that as she laid on her back on the wild grasses of the shelf, energy levels all but extinguished from the climb, Kwan forgot why she was there just for a moment as she marveled at its magnificence. Near the peak of Hokkenzen Mountain the sky was clear. One of the clouds reached high in the sky in a shape not unlike a wild unicorn reared on its hind legs, a shape more massive than anything she'd ever seen before save the mountain it passed over. It caught the same oranges of the sunset, which made it look even more majestic. She watched the cloud as it slowly shifted and faded into an unrecognizable mass.

They were so tired that they decided to spend the night under the stars. Kwan insisted Hanzo get up and lay down fifty paces away to which he reluctantly agreed. Not for wanting to be near her, but because the effort to stand up and trudge even that little distance was akin to sprinting across long miles of grassland fully rested. When he reached a suitably dry spot he collapsed on the ground and fell asleep immediately. Similarly, Kwan passed out. Tiger Claw had calmed down since they reached the shelf but still exuded warmth. It's as if it knew she was cold.

When she awoke the next morning, Hanzo still snored fast asleep. Luckily there wasn't anyone else around as far as the eye could see in this desolate grassland. The wind was strong and it rustled the grass in a way that sounded like heavy rain hitting the ground. She stood and brushed the grass off herself. She noticed Tiger Claw rumble again as she reached down and picked it up off the ground. She strapped it to her hip. It rumbled more furiously now. It rumbled so much it even made the sound of a bee with each pulse.

"What's wrong, Tiger Claw? I wish you could tell me." When she looked up over the grassland at the snowy, looming mountain in the distance, it rumbled out of control and shook the sheath with it wildly. It jolted her off her feet and caused her to fall to her knees. Then it calmed. She held the sword before her and like a babe that returned to its mother's arms it quieted to a low buzz. She looked to the mountain again and it gave two stiff shakes as if to say *No, no not there. Anywhere but there.*

"That's where we're going, Tiger Claw. And if I die, I die. One way or another, I'll be with Unomichi again. In life, or in death."

Hanzo was awake now. He brushed himself off and attached his pair of swords to his hip under his dusty brown robes. "Everything alright, Kwan?" he called as he trotted over to her.

She tucked the sword against her hip, "Yes, everything's fine. We should be going."

"One detail I neglected to mention," he began. "We'll reach the path at the end of this grassland. It passes near Opporo and there's a possibility we will run into an armed patrol. We may need to solve this problem creatively," he double-tapped the hilt of his katana. "Once we're past the city I will part ways with you. That's as far as I'll go." She nodded in understanding. The two of them walked together and put the ocean waters of the bay behind them.

There was very little else besides grass on the shelf. There was a tree far to the left whose branches full of green needles stretched wider than the tree was tall. It got cold. Very cold. And before long the cloud cover obscured the sun and snow flurries threatened to layer the pristinely green grass. Before they made it to the dirt path Kwan could see the tracks she left behind in the frost. Tiger Claw kept her warm but Hanzo clearly suffered. She did not want to tell him she carried a legendary sword though. The less he knew the better. Still, she kept quiet and feigned shivering to avert his suspicion.

Along the decades-old pathway, which was not as perturbed by the frost, they came around a hilly section along the north side. Then she saw it: the staunch walls of Opporo Castle. Soon she saw the drab, murky moat at its foot. The path ran along the moat the rest of its length. Over the battlements she could see men busily fixing the walls in a high level of the otherwise impressive pagoda tower.

Hanzo pointed, "That must be where the dragon attacked. I heard it blew all the walls of the entire level out. A huge wonder that it didn't knock over the whole thing."

Kwan told him, her jaw tight, "I know the man that did it. He's the reason I came here." *I shouldn't have told him that.*

Hanzo's eyebrows jumped up his forehead. "You mean to say you're here to hunt him down? I heard it was a man named Ryu or Riku or something and he summoned the dragon out of thin air!"

"Essentially yes. I'm hunting him down. I know I'll find him at Hokkenzen Shrine. That's where I'll make my move."

215

"You'd have to be a strong warrior to defeat him. Do you think you're ready?"

She thought for a moment before she responded and blinked a long, heavy blink. Then she said, "I'll have to be. I have no other choice. It's me that lives, or him."

He huffed in disbelief and shook his head as if he travelled alongside a dead man walking. "I'd think it's astoundingly crazy to challenge someone that powerful. But you're not paying me for my life advice; you're paying me to guide you, and guiding you I am." With that they continued up the path in solemn silence. They reached close enough to the mountain that the ground began to incline.

After more walking, Hanzo said, "We're nearly out of reach of the patrols. Thankfully we didn't come across any—wait I hear something. Quick, behind the bushes!" Tiger Claw rumbled heavily now. They scurried behind a dense bush as a lone, large, armored patrolman marched past. He had them at his back when he halted in his tracks. Kwan tried her best to quiet the rumbles but it was no use. The patrolman pointed his lance directly at them.

"You! The roads are closed. Get back to the city. *Now!*" His yell held an unexpected ferocity that made Kwan jump.

"Sir, we're merely passing through," Hanzo said. "Mistress, give him some money for his trouble."

Without thinking she took her entire coin purse and tossed it meekly at the patrolman's feet. He picked it up and shoved it in a pocket beneath his breastplate. "Thanks for the coin. Now back to the city with ye." He stepped toward them and hit the butt of his spear on the ground.

"Creativity," Hanzo reminded her. He leapt out onto the path and addressed the patrolman calmly. "My name is

216

Nakamura Hanzo. I'm a samurai of Hakazu. It seems we are at an impasse." Before another word he revealed his katana and pulled it out. Though the white handle was worn with sweat, the blade was in pristine condition. "Now that you know my name, I can't let you live."

"My name is Shigure Kenzo. And you've made a challenge to a royal patrolman. Your final mistake of what I presume to be a collection of many."

Hanzo spoke to Kwan but his eyes never left Kenzo's. "Always give the man you're about to slay the decency of letting him know the name of his killer. You only die a warrior once, after all." He addressed his opponent, "I am the bearer of the name of a long line of samurai warriors, Kenzo-san. I was taught swordplay by my grandfather, Nakamura Hitei, who was a pupil of the honorable Hattori Hanzo himself. I do not like your chances."

Kwan ran a little further up the path and turned around to watch. She had no idea Hanzo's skill level, whether he was a master of swordplay or a fool that swung around a metal stick and threw around names of legendary samurai. She hoped it was the former.

Hanzo inched toward Kenzo and kept the same foot forward. He never removed his eyes from his opponent's. He made a fade and the spearman nudged. Hanzo kept his distance. He began to circle slowly to his right. He knew it would make it trickier for a lance thrust to land. Hanzo paused as the spearman's back was to Kwan. The men stared each other down for twenty focused breaths. Hanzo waited for his chance. He knew that when Kenzo's eyes broke contact would be the moment he struck. The chilly breeze blew Hanzo's robes, but the man was unmoved and refused to let go of his stare. Kwan breathed heavily and Tiger

Claw's rumbles thickened. It shook so furiously that it bothered her to hold the handle.

Kenzo lost his patience. His eyes briefly dropped to Hanzo's feet and at that moment he leapt forward and thrusted. Hanzo swatted the spear to his left and put a hand on the shaft. He spun and turned his katana close to himself at throat level until he outstretched his blade and slashed the spearman at the weak spot of the neck. The patrolman dropped his metal weapon to the ground. Blood spurted from his severed artery. He grasped at the bleeding wound and fell over before he lost consciousness and died choking on a pool of his own blood.

"The end of Shigure Kenzo," Hanzo said to the dead man. "Rest in peace, fellow wanderer." He removed a cloth from his back pocket and gently cleaned off the bit of blood along the edge of his sword blade. He rubbed it until it was perfectly reflective again as if he shined a shoe. Then he put it back in its sheath and dragged the patrolman behind the same bush they had hidden behind. Kwan said nothing. She blankly watched him do this.

Hanzo said, "Now the matter of my payment—"

"Check the dead man."

"You gave him my payment?!"

"I remember you mentioning creativity?" she said. He grimaced and pulled the coin purse out of the dead man's pocket.

"Keep the whole purse. It's yours," she said.

"This is a vast overpayment, Kwan-san."

"I may have no use for it anyway after this."

He smiled. "If I see you again back in Hakazu, I'll buy you a famous Opporo beer."

She gave him a half smile full of gratitude, "That won't be necessary. Use that money to fix up your katana. It's filthy."

218

"You sound like Shogo-san. I'm a bit more concerned with functionality than beauty."

Kwan raised an eyebrow and said, "That's apparent. Take care of yourself Hanzo-san. I'll continue alone from here."

His tone shifted from playfulness to serious concern. "Please be careful. Come back alive."

She thought for a second and tracked her eyes up the mountain path. She turned and blinked slowly. "I promise."

/ / /

Their fireplace cast a flickering glow in their shared bedroom as they tried to sleep. Akari felt the gem on her necklace. Ever since Mizu gave it to her, she hadn't taken it off. It was the only gift anyone had given her since she left Iga Temple. As she laid there on her bed roll with Mizu fast asleep on her own, she could not help but smile. She needed to replace the leather cord that held the gem soon. She practically had to beg Daisuke-sensei to let her wear it during training. He relented, finally, though not before he scolded her before the rest of the pupils. She didn't care though. It's not as if they would exile her into the forest.

She looked over to her very much asleep friend. "Mizu. Hey, Mizu-chan, wake up."

Mizu sighed, barely awake. She shifted under the covers. "What is it, Akari-chan? Spirits, it's so late."

"Mizu-chan, I can't sleep. I'm nervous about the blue belt test tomorrow. I...I don't know if I'm ready for it."

Mizu grunted, "Yeah you'll probably fall flat on your face during the *kata* in front of everyone." Akari smiled and chuckled to herself. Mizu loved to tease her. "You're already a yellow belt.

219

You'll do fine Akari-chan. You're almost as good as me. Almost."

"Almost," Akari said with a side eye.

"Before you know it you'll be a black belt. Now shut up. It's too late," Mizu said.

"You shut up," Akari snapped back.

"I'm trying! Now go to sleep." Before long Mizu passed out. Akari turned her head toward the window. The stars were beautiful tonight in the clear winter night sky. She could even see her favorite constellation. The Tigress pulled the north star with her tail. Unlike some of the other constellations that had only a vague similarity to their namesake, this one resembled the outline of a tiger closely. Soon she drifted off to sleep.

Chapter 26

•••

Hanzo-san is so attractive. I hate myself for even thinking it though. What would Gung Lao think if I suddenly gave up and settled down after coming this far? He'd storm off and never speak to me again after all I put him through. Hanzo is a ruffian. A samurai sure, but a destitute one. Kwan was lost in thought as she trudged along the snow-covered path. She had hiked uphill for hours and the path only grew steeper. Tiger Claw had not stopped its low rumbling. She would soon need to set up camp. The stars and waning moon lit up the snowy mountainside. She decided to hike through the night. The sooner she reached the apex, the sooner it would all be over for Riku, or for herself, though she shuddered at the thought.

She hardly noticed the cold. Thanks to Tiger Claw's warmth, it felt to her like a breezy spring day. She was aware of the relative ease she was having when it came to the temperature and assumed it was because of the sword. What else could it be?

We're nearly there, Tiger Claw. We're nearly there she thought as she tried to soothe the shaking weapon. If the sword was alive, it certainly was nervous. *You must have a sentient spirit inside you, don't you? What else could it be? It's okay. We'll make it through this.* She continued to smooth the handle as she trudged up the mountain.

221

The snow-covered dirt path had long since petered out and she now hiked on snowy ridgeline. It was untrodden. Up ahead she noticed something she was waiting for.

Yes! There it is! The first torii gate. She quickened her pace towards the solitary archway that marked the path to the shrine. The red paint of the lonely gate had long since faded and chipped in many places which revealed the wooden structure. Finally, she passed through it. It reminded her of a similar one near her home at Iga Temple. As she put the gate behind her the clouds of the night sky faded and the bright stars lit the path even more brilliantly. It was a breathtaking sight. The constellation of the Tigress made its way closer to the mountain peak while it pulled the north star with its tail. She watched it as she continued her journey up the mountain. The wind died down and she felt a new sense of revitalization encourage her to push on.

/ / /

Riku slipped out of his room without waking Hiriko or Kasume. He left everything except Dragon Fang and his knapsack with a few provisions. He double-checked that he remembered the bone scroll as well. The sun had not even begun to relinquish the night, yet he had no choice but to leave now. Kasume and Hiriko could not make it up the mountain in their condition and he wouldn't want them to anyway. To bring his late wife back to life was a personal matter to him and they would get in his way. The innkeeper's plump middle-aged wife wordlessly watched him head out of the inn. She had no indication of where he was headed though she knew better than to question a Koga ninja.

He stopped as he reached the doorway and looked over his shoulder at her. "My companions will cover the costs. Tell them I left without them and I will not be returning. Tell them to go home. Goodbye," he said. Without waiting for her response, which she did not offer, he left.

It was cold. Brutally cold. At least he had thought ahead and bought warm clothes with some of the dwindling coin they had remaining. Still, he felt the bitter cutting chill. The snow on the path out of Opporo so far was already ankle-deep. As he trudged further up the path, he tried to remember the warmth of Yuuki's touch. He imagined himself with her on a warm summer day as they wasted time by the river and dipped their feet in the chilly rushing water. It was a sweet feeling. He closed his eyes and took a deep breath. He let it out slowly and imagined her beautiful long hair, soft skin, and glowing smile. He tried to fend off the thoughts that he was making a mistake.

The further he went up the path, the steeper the incline became. Weariness began to take hold as the dirt of the path became sparser. The trees along the path thinned too and ahead there was only more hiking left to do. He trudged step after step and often wished he had never come to this mountain. His calves ached and his back grew weary. Ahead he saw something. It was the first torii gate. Under the gate he noticed one set of fresh footprints in a thin layer of snow. *There's…someone else on the mountain.* Thoughts ran through his mind of the dream he had. The woman before the shrine that wore a tiger's mask looked over her shoulder at him. *Is it Yuuki? My Yuuki-chan?* The thought of her quickened his pace.

As he went he could not take his eyes off the footprints. They led further up the ridge. Before long, he passed under the second torii gate. Each gust of wind chilled him to the bone. The stars in the dragon's constellation zig-zagged to the east of the mountain and began to hide below the horizon, though all the stars gradually faded as the sun rose. For an hour he marched alone up the path, then another. He tossed his eaten apple core to the side and pressed on. With the sun halfway up the clear skies, the mountain slope was steep now. His thighs fiercely burned and his ankles tightened but thoughts of Yuuki coming back to him kept him going. Her being alive would likely complicate things with Sakura, but he desperately wanted her back regardless.

Higher and higher the Koga ninja climbed. The air grew thinner. Another torii gate stood ahead. The incline softened. Spaced, engraved stone slabs formed steps, a huge relief to the tired climber. He quickened his stride.

And there it was—he could see the frozen stone overhang of Hokkenzen Shrine beyond the final torii gate. The path rounded an icy wall that obscured his vision of the small plaza before the altar. Exhausted, he made the final steps under the stone gate. And there she was, the lone woman in his vision.

She stood there alone before the altar. The enclosure, carved from natural stone into the mountainside just beneath the summit, looked centuries old and was frozen over ten-fold. There was a barren stone table fit to hold offerings, though it looked as if the woman neglected to leave anything. Her black robes with vermillion flower print were uncharacteristically light for the weather near the summit of a mountain, although she appeared unperturbed.

His step crunched the snow-covered gravel and she glanced back over her shoulder at the sound. She looked back to the altar and said, "Finally, you've come. I've been waiting for you."

"Kwan-san. What are you doing here? You're hundreds of miles from home. I expected to come here alone, yet here you are."

She grinned to herself, her back still to him. She gave a single clap to the shrine and bowed to it deeper than she ever had before in her life. When she straightened again she covered the handle of her sword and turned toward Riku. "Yet here I am," she said. A fierce look fell upon her face.

Shocked at her fiery countenance, Riku said, "Kwan-san, you've come all this way. Why? I had a feeling I was being followed, but I did not expect it to be you. What's happened?"

"You know in your heart what you've done and why I'm here." She spit to the ground, unladylike from Riku's point of view. "The night of the battle, *you killed Unomichi-san without mercy. Without even a second thought! You murdered him! Tell me why! Explain yourself!*"

Riku was aghast. He was shocked she had this strong of an emotional reaction to him, strong enough to follow him to the peak of a remote mountain. "I did what had to be done in the moment. The demons. They were destroying the temple! He was caught in the way. I was saddened by his death more than you could imag—"

"*SPIRITS!*" she interrupted. "*You didn't care at ALL about his death! And you brutally murdered him!*"

225

Riku was taken aback. He replied, "Watch your tone before the spirits, Kwan-san! This is the most serious of accusations! What do you intend to do?"

At that she pulled out Tiger Claw and put on a straight face. She paced to the far end of the shrine, turned, and faced him down. She said flatly, "You will bring him back to life. And then I will kill you. And that will be the end of it." Tiger Claw rumbled more strongly than ever. It set itself ablaze. The blade glowed orange as if newly cast.

"I can't do that. I've come to revive my late wife. She is more important to me than he is." He uncovered the handle of Dragon Fang and grasped it. "That sword. Tiger Claw. It no longer belongs to you. I am confiscating it as your wild demeanor proves you can no longer be trusted to wield it. And it saddens me greatly to learn you've come all this way just to attempt to assassinate me."

"*Enough of your snake talk*," she bit back. "You will submit to me and *bring him back! Or I'll kill you! I'm warning you!*"

"You leave me no choice. If you are truly committed to this fight, Kwan, I will defend myself." He took his place on the opposite side of the shrine, tossing his knapsack next to the altar.

"Dropping the honorifics, I see. You truly are a snake!" Tiger Claw's glow made her sweat and loosen her faltering grip of the handle, though she tightened and stood still. Riku pulled Dragon Fang out only an inch. He revealed the dragon engravement that bared its wings and breathed fire. It glowed a blinding violet luster. He gripped the handle and stood unmoved, then assumed a ready stance.

The wind picked up. It gusted the flames of the orange sword nearer to Kwan's face though she was unperturbed. She felt the anger well up inside her to its boiling point. It was all she could do to keep calm. She breathed hard. This was it, the moment she had waited for.

The two stood several paces apart, outside of each other's range. Riku's eyes remained closed. He didn't need to make the first move. No, she was going to attack. Any moment now.

As he predicted she screamed wildly and thrust herself toward him, the burning sword's flames trailed. But Riku's eyes remained closed. The sword remained in its sheath. Time slowed for him and he could count her steps. *Ichi. Ni. San. Shi.* As expected, she wildly launched herself at him. When she was one pace from his range he opened his eyes and unsheathed his legendary sword. He stepped to the side and watched her overhead strike find nothing but air. He swung at her but she turned around just in time and blocked, knocking her back. She regained her footing and tried again. He blocked the overhead strike.

To their surprise, a tiger spirit sprouted from the flames. The spirit was massive. Its ephemeral body was translucent and it glowed with a bright vermillion luster. Riku could do nothing but take a long leap backwards to avoid the tiger's swipe. There she was between them, the Tigress defending her kin.

"Tigress! You are meant to defend this sword, not attack it! Back away!" Riku pleaded. The tiger spirit stalked slowly toward him. "You will regret this, if you survive, Tigress."

He shut his eyes again, held Dragon Fang in both hands, and pointed it towards the heavens. A ring of purple flames encircled

Riku on the ground two paces around him. A violet light shot up and spread. *Noroi no Owari*, the legendary spirit dragon, emerged from the glow. It surveyed the scene, already aware of the situation. Its massive claws touched the ground and its glow enveloped Riku. The tiger spirit focused and launched itself at the spirit dragon which took it over the side of the mountain while both ninjas watched. Soon the spirits appeared but it was the dragon holding the tiger. It lifted it high into the air and dropped it directly over the mountain peak.

Seizing the opportunity, Kwan took her burning sword and charged Riku. He swatted her back again. He ran across the shrine to the path that led up to the summit. She chased after him. The tiger's fall was broken when it crushed the shrine plaza, before the altar. It shook off the harm and roared a fiery breath up at the dragon. The dragon dove at it and let loose a heavy blast of violet holy fire down onto the spirit animal below. The cat protected itself with a barrier before the dragon came crashing down upon it.

Riku was too preoccupied to witness the carnage. He was at the narrow summit of Hokkenzen Mountain. The only thing that marked it was a waist high stone monument of a Buddha that faced the eastern horizon with one palm raised to greet the sunrise. The sunshine up here blinded them with zero cloud cover. Riku would have passed out from exhaustion and thin air had the adrenaline in his blood not kept him fighting. He countered Kwan's strikes with Dragon Fang, its purple mist fizzled from the blade and its emblem glowed blindingly.

Blow after blow he countered. He offered many swings of his own which were countered in return. *This could be it, my final battle. I am so tired and she will not back down. She fights with such animalistic ferocity. I don't know how much longer I can last.* His back was to a drop to the shrine below where the spirits were fighting. He saw the Tigress swing a mighty swipe on the dragon.

Kwan swung and he blocked and countered. Finally, she swung a particularly strong downwards strike at him to which he narrowly sidestepped. In a flash he shoved her and there was no ground beneath her. She toppled over the edge and dropped the burning sword. Tiger Claw lodged itself point down into the ground below and stood tall. She barely caught the ledge with one hand. She looked up at Riku and met his gaze. In that moment a wave of burning regret washed over her as she closed her eyes. He reached down to pull her up but she was so exhausted that she let go and fell to the ground below. Time stood still as she fell and the last thing she saw was Riku reaching down after her. In the last moment she reached back to him as she fell through the battling spirit animals.

Riku shut his eyes just before she landed. It was not pretty. The spirit dragon saw an opening and grabbed onto the tiger. It lifted it off the mountainside. The tiger struggled helplessly. The dragon swung back around toward the shrine and when it neared it, it let go. The tiger crashed into the shrine's overhang and destroyed it. Riku leapt out of the way and landed back onto the path. Hokkenzen Mountain now stood twenty feet shorter, the rocky summit tumbled down the rear mountainside. The Tiger gave one last roar before it vanished amongst the rubble. The offering table was miraculously untouched.

229

Noroi no Owari swung around and landed itself on the rubble near where the tiger spirit disappeared. It gave one last fierce roar and blasted the sky with holy fire. It turned to Riku on the path and motioned toward the offering table. The dragon looked up to the sun before it vanished as a cloudy mist in the wind.

Chapter 27

Dying Breath

Riku hurried down around the summit path which, behind him, led to nowhere. He went to her side. She was still breathing, however shallowly and laid in blood. Tiger Claw stood and glowed as it tried to burn a hole through the mountain.

"Kwan-san! Come on! We need to leave this place while we still can," he cried desperately. Never had he shed tears for an opponent this fiercely before. He wrapped his arms around her as she lay dying.

Her eyes opened a crack. "Riku-san...I completed my mission...Now, at least, I'll finally be with my love Unomichi once again." She coughed blood. "Leave me to die. I want to be with him once again." Her eyes looked up to the blue sky above them, and her life left her.

Riku didn't know he had it in him to moan as strongly and as desperately as he did but the moan did come.

I...I must choose. I must choose. He struggled over to his knapsack. The destruction had uncovered a pedestal where a sword made of clear crystal ice rested on a stone rack. He gave it only a passing glance as he rifled into his knapsack.

Where is it? Where is the bone scroll? Where is it? He tossed out everything else until he found the hide wrappings that held the bundle of bones. He unwrapped them and revealed the scroll. The illegible text that was scratched down the bones glowed a cyan luster. *I'm here. At the altar. Oh, Spirits I'm here. But who do I choose? Yuuki? Or Unomichi? Spirits, I was so sure. But what of Kwan? What would Unomichi think if I revived him and the first thing he saw was his love lying dead before him? He'd throw himself off the mountain! He'd want me to save her. Yes, I must save her. Yuuki…I'm sorry…I will join you again…one day…*

Tears welled up in his eyes. He stood and placed the scroll onto the frozen stone offering table. He took a step back and clapped twice. He bowed low.

"Spirits. Oh, Great Spirits of the afterlife. Oh, sublime creators. With this offering I ask you to bring her back to life. Please bring Kwan back to life. Please. I beg you!"

The glowing text pulsed. The symbols left the scroll and appeared before the altar. The angular characters were ancient, completely illegible to him. A voice rang in his head. It said with booming clarity, "You choose Kwan to be resurrected? Remember, only one may be brought back. Is this your final choice?"

Riku shut his eyes and a tear fought its way out of each one. "Yes. She is my choice. Bring her back to life, oh Spirit of the mountain."

"Very well, Riku-san. In a moment, she will breathe life anew." The voice said no more. The letters came together and weaved themselves into a ribbon. The ribbon fluttered its way to Kwan and disappeared into her chest. As she coughed awake Riku noticed the crystal sword sitting in the rubble. He climbed over the stones and gently took it up. It was cold to the touch and it looked as if it would melt at any second.

A voice in his head told him its title. He said it aloud to himself: "Bear's Bite." He had barely a moment to inspect it when he heard Kwan's crying. She wept inconsolably. But it was not out of pain. It was out of sorrow.

"I saw him, Riku-san!" she cried. "I held him! I kissed him! My Unomichi! Why am I back? Why am I alive again? Tell me why?!"

He looked back down to Bear's Bite in his hands. There it was; the chill. "I brought you back because it was not your time to die. At least not yet." She eased onto her back and looked up at the sun directly above, blinding as ever. Riku stood silently as she wept. Before long, he said, "You have been sent back because your mission is not yet complete. A great war is coming. A war for humanity. Do you feel it?"

She remained silent for a moment but then said, "Yes. I know it is coming. Is it…the demon lord?"

"Yes. He means to take over the human realm. His power is building. You must help me stop him before it is too late."

"You wasted your one chance on someone as pathetic as me. Why?"

"Unomichi would have me bring you back instead of himself," he said. "You know this to be true." He walked over to the edge of the demolished shrine plaza to the south. From there he could just make out the shores of Honshu Island on the horizon and the rest of Japan beyond. The view was the most beautiful sight he had ever seen. "I can't do it alone," he said into the distance. "You are the wielder of a legendary sword. And I need your help."

Kwan brought herself up and brushed the bloody snow off her legs. She brusquely snatched Tiger Claw with one hand. She went to him. She looked at the sword, its glow died down but for the triple claw mark engravement on the blade above the guard.

"Kwan, if you swear to follow me, I promise I will find another way to bring Unomichi back to life. I just need you to forgive me. It was never my intention to kill him. He was like a brother to me."

Kwan breathed hard and looked at the claw marks. They pulsed, though the sword did not shake as it did before. "I have your word?" He kept his eyes on the horizon and nodded. She squeezed her eyes tight as if she swallowed down all the emotion she felt in the time since Unomichi's death. She presented the sword horizontally as she knelt, bowing.

"I give my oath to you, Riku-sama. To serve under you and defend the realm. In exchange, you will find a way to bring Unomichi back to life."

Riku turned to look at her and asked, "Until your dying breath?"

She grinned. "Until my dying breath, and beyond." At that he smiled and she did too. She stood and they bowed to each other.

As they turned to look at the view, Riku thought he caught a glimmer of the constellations of both the Tigress and the Dragon. "We have a long journey back."

"There is a stop I need to make in Hakazu if we can. Oh, and another in Omamori."

Riku thought for a second and said, "Sure."

The blade of the frozen sword, Bear's Bite, was melting as he held it. The ice of the handle became as opaque as snow. Riku flicked it and the frost fell off. It revealed a solid white woven handle.

"What's that?" Kwan asked.

"It's a legendary sword. It's called *Bear's Bite*."

"I've never heard of it before," she said.

"Neither have I," Riku admitted. "Come now. Let's make our return." And with that, they began their long trek down the mountain. Back home.

/ / /

Thank you for reading.

Stay tuned for Volume III of

Dragon Fang and Tiger Claw

www.ingramcontent.com/pod-product-compliance
Lightning Source LLC
Chambersburg PA
CBHW060634260626
47161CB00008B/2889